I0524707

The Heart of St. Nick

A.D. ELLIS

CHAPTER 1

Gannon Joseph Snow

"Gannon, be reasonable," Shan said, all but stomping his foot as he crossed his arms over his chest in my bedroom. "You can't possibly think I'm going to be okay with you *leaving* for some Podunk little Santa Claus town in the Midwest right before Christmas."

Sighing, and not at all upset with his temper tantrum because I'd known where this relationship was going—or not going—for the past month—I continued to pack my suitcase.

My long-time assistant, Ellen, had taken care of booking my flight and ride to the airport. I didn't have a lot of time to dawdle.

"It's called Saint Nicholas Crossing. I may be back before Christmas." I slipped past him to grab one more pair of jeans, another t-shirt, and a sweater. I knew the Midwest was cold this time of year, and I didn't exactly have a plethora of winter-wear, but I didn't think my usual dress pants and Oxford with a tie were going to cut it.

"We had plans!" Shan said, this time actually stomping his foot.

"No, *you* had plans." I pointed my finger at his pretty face. "I told you when we started this thing I didn't have time for a relationship and I didn't do sentimental or holidays. It's not my fault you didn't listen and thought you could change me."

Shan was gorgeous with his bleach-blond hair, sun-kissed skin, and full lips—all of which he paid *very* well for. But he was just one more in a line of pretty, young twinks I'd been attempting to scratch an itch with over the past however many years.

At thirty-seven, after several failed relationships, maybe it was time to swear off men for good—especially the young twinks.

I just wasn't cut out for love.

Or I was looking in the wrong places.

Or...

Blah, blah, blah.

Maybe I was just a grumpy asshole who didn't deserve to find love.

I didn't really like a lot of people, maybe it was best for me to be alone.

"Ganny," Shan said, pout filling his puffy lips.

"Stop, you know I hate that name."

"Damn it, Gannon." Shan tried again. "I have parties lined up. I need you here."

"That was one of your many mistakes. I don't do parties. I wasn't fucking you to be your arm-candy." I zipped up my suitcase and held out my hand. "Give me the key you've been using."

Shan had the decency to look confused.

"The one you had made when you think I didn't realize you'd taken mine? I need it back unless you're planning to come gather my mail and check on my plants while I'm gone."

He wrinkled his nose and fished in his pocket.

Slamming the key into my hand, Shan pursed his lips. "You're going to regret this. When you get back from Timbuktu and want a piece of ass, I won't be around."

"Yeah, kinda figured that."

"For real, Gannon, we're breaking up."

"Again, I got it. I wish you all the best, Shan. I really do. I'm sorry I couldn't be more what you were looking for."

I'm sorry I couldn't be what anyone was looking for.

But really, who wanted a thirty-seven-year-old grumpy realtor with a frozen heart the size of a postage stamp?

I knew my faults and I wasn't what most would describe as a catch.

Sure, I had a successful job and money wasn't an issue.

And I supposed I looked good, but looks only got a person so far.

The silver at my temples mixing in with jet black hair didn't make up for my grumpy personality and lack of a heart.

The shot of silver in the five o'clock shadow along my strong jawline and glint of my grey-blue eyes didn't excuse my complete disdain for most people on most days.

At just over six-feet and well-built, I commanded a room and almost always got what I wanted when it came to men and real-estate deals, but I wasn't someone a lot of people thought fondly of.

And that was fine by me.

If it left me a bit lonely from time to time, I dealt with it.

I was a successful realtor in one of the biggest cities in the world, I really didn't have much to complain about.

Or, more accurately, I had plenty to complain and be sad about, but I didn't allow it. There was no good to come of it and wishing for things to be different was just a waste of valuable time.

I followed Shan to the parking lot of my condo

community and watched him stomp his way to his little hybrid, grateful he wasn't making more of a scene.

Five minutes later, I tossed my suitcase in the back of my ride and headed toward LAX.

Was it bad I wasn't even the slightest bit upset about Shan?

He wasn't a bad guy, just over-the-top materialistic and much too worried about what people thought of him.

The sex had been good—but most sex was at least decent. True, I didn't really believe claims of life-altering sex and soul-deep connections, but I was satisfied with a sexy, warm body under me in bed. I didn't *need* the connection or fireworks in the bedroom.

Could I have *maybe* waited until after the holidays to travel to Saint Nicholas Crossing and take care of the sale of my late grandfather's home and business?

Yeah, most likely.

Did a part of me know I'd opted to travel right before the holidays knowing Shan would freak out and leave?

Again, yes.

But the sooner I got to Christmas town and took care of my grandfather's estate, the sooner I'd be back in sunny Los Angeles.

Los Angeles.

The smog.

The traffic.

The people.

God, so many people.

I'd contemplated the fact I was feeling a bit trapped—suffocated—in LA lately.

The urge to flee had been slowly building.

But where would I go?

Aside from a few extended trips to Saint Nicholas Crossing as a kid and teen, I'd never *lived* anywhere but LA.

Sure, I'd done a lot of traveling, but I'd always returned to sunny LA.

As I watched the crowded city-scape pass outside the window of my ride, I wondered again if a change was needed.

I was one of the most successful realtors in the area, but I could easily work pretty much anywhere if I put my mind to it.

Maybe once I returned from St. Nicholas Crossing and the hubbub from the holidays died down, I'd take a look at potential locations for a move.

Somewhere I didn't have a thousand people within a hundred feet everywhere I turned.

Somewhere I could hole up and be anti-social if I damn well pleased.

Until then, I'd be dealing with the folks in St. Nicholas Crossing—a small railroad town with streets named after reindeer and citizens with more heart than money.

As a child, I'd been in love with the place. And I'd adored my grandfather, who was the kindest, most cheerful, loving man I'd ever met, unlike his asshole son.

As a teen, more and more angry and jaded each and every day as my parents' marriage fell apart and trapped me in the middle of their vicious fights, I'd still loved escaping to St. Nicholas Crossing and my grandfather.

But each passing year found me more and more closed off to the whimsical magic and cheery joy of the little town, until I finally stopped going to see Grandpa because it was easier to shut it all out.

As my car pulled up to the drop-off lane at the airport, I sent up a prayer to whoever was listening that my excursion would be quick and painless.

A house and a store.

Those were the two things my late grandfather, Joseph Snow, had left to me.

With my skills and a bit of luck, I'd be out of St. Nicholas Crossing and sipping a cocktail on my balcony by Christmas Eve.

In and out.

No need for nostalgia.

No room for sentimentality.

St. Nicholas Crossing was from my long-ago past. Hell, I'd lost touch with Grandpa beyond a birthday card and yearly letter from him for the past decade—and damn if my gut didn't sour with guilt over that one. I'd always sent him a gift on his birthday along with a card, but the part of me that still had a heart recognized a phone call or a visit would have meant more.

The man was the only family I'd claimed after my parents divorced and moved on—I hadn't spoken to them since I was eighteen—and the news of their deaths a couple years apart, Mom from too much partying and drugs, Dad from a heart attack, hadn't even made me blink.

But my heart still hurt to know Grandpa Joseph was gone.

Shaking my head and huffing out a breath, I pushed aside the silly emotions. There was no time or reason for getting upset. What was done, was done. I had a job to do, nothing more. Getting sentimental about my late grandfather would only churn up more guilt and wasn't productive.

Making a beeline toward my gate—the familiar anxiousness over flying coursing through my veins—I gave brief consideration to calling Ellen to let her know I'd be making a road trip out of my return to LA. I'd wrap things up with my grandfather's estate, rent a car, and spend a week sight-seeing to clear my head as I journeyed back to the City of Angels.

Either way, as much as I wanted to feel bad about Shan, all I felt was relieved.

I needed a break from dating.

A break from young, pretty guys.

It wasn't as if I was looking for love—quite the opposite, in fact.

I took men home for sex.

If they opted to stay and make things into more, that was their decision—and mistake.

I just wasn't cut out for a relationship—not made for love.

My parents had made sure I couldn't keep a healthy relationship going.

I had no family near me or living.

And that was fine by me—I didn't need the entanglement.

Taking a deep breath as I boarded the plane, I decided this little trip and task would be a nice break and a good refresh.

A bit of time *roughing it* in a small town would be the reset I needed.

The bone-chilling cold and icy slush of snow would be just what I needed to really appreciate what I had in LA.

If the thought of returning to LA had a tiny pit of dread forming in my gut, it would likely dissipate by the time my excursion neared its end. I'd be longing for the sunshine and anonymity of the big city in no time flat.

Swoop in, put the estate in order, sell, and walk away.

That was the plan.

No falling prey to memories.

No letting my heart recall how happy the place used to make me.

No Christmas cheer.

I could do it. I'd been blocking people out, walls up around my heart, for over two decades. Hell, my grandpa wasn't even *there* anymore. Not letting myself feel anything would be even easier.

This was business only.

And looking on the positive side, at least I wouldn't have to worry about any cute, young twinks in St. Nicholas Crossing.

CHAPTER 2

Hayden Christopher Green

"ENJOY YOUR WEEKEND, CANDY," I said with a smile and a wave to one of St. Nicholas Crossing's oldest and most beloved citizens. "You too, Ginger," I added when the other woman stuck her head around the corner.

Candy and Ginger were inseparable.

They'd been living in St. Nick's their entire lives—with the exception of the years they tried to move away—and had plenty of stories to tell to anyone who took time to listen, and maybe even those who didn't.

As the head cooks at the small K-12 school, the women knew absolutely every single person in our tiny town.

"You too, Hayden. Maybe get yourself a hot date," Candy said with a wicked grin.

I laughed. "Hot dates aren't plentiful around here." Waving a stack of papers before stuffing them in my bag, I said, "Plus, I've got papers to grade and plenty to do at the store. No time for dates."

Nestled smack dab in the hills of the Midwest, St. Nicholas Crossing was a tiny railroad town. Not a lot of money, but plenty of holiday cheer year-round. With a very small school to educate approximately two-hundred-fifty children, the town did its best with what we had.

As a part-time teacher at the school, I split my day between teaching three classes of middle school and high school English and helping my dad run The Heart of St. Nicholas, also known as St. Nick's Heart, the general store that truly was the heart of our town.

My parents had lived most of their lives in the Crossing. They'd moved away to go to college, but returned after graduation and had no plans to leave.

My mom, Carol Green, did most of the work when it came to fundraising, writing grants, and reaching out to organizations and resources to help the town. With a degree in social work and philanthropy, she was the best at what she did for our citizens. The fact she wore a perpetual smile between her rosy cheeks, organized the Christmas carolers every year, and never met a person who didn't need a hug made her a natural when it came to making everyone in town feel welcome, safe, and cared for.

Dad, Jack Green, oversaw every aspect of the general store. Right in the middle of town, the store was as much a hub as the railroad was. While the railroad provided several jobs, the store provided jobs, goods, and survival for many in town. Dad put his business and social work degrees to good use as he ran the store.

Neither of my parents were making big bucks, but they had money coming in from small inheritances, past investments, and their very humble salaries. The thing about St. Nicholas Crossing was we maybe weren't rolling in the dough, but we also lived modestly with a very low cost of living, and we were beyond rich when it came to taking care of our own, sense of community, and general cheer.

Myself, I'd grown up in the town—never really realizing there was life outside St. Nick's—gone off to college, earned a degree, tried to live elsewhere, but got pulled back in by the tiny town.

The place wasn't for everyone.

Some folks were there because it was the only job they could get thanks to life circumstances beyond their control.

Others had nowhere else to go.

Many, like my parents and me, chose to stay in St. Nick's because it was where our hearts felt the most at home.

So, between teaching—which I adored—and helping with the store—which I loved almost even more—my heart and schedule were full.

That didn't mean I didn't long for love.

I did.

Very much so.

But it would take a Christmas miracle of epic proportions to make that happen.

Not that I didn't believe in such things, I very much did.

However, my heart was in St. Nicholas Crossing and we didn't get a lot of single gay men coming to town.

Sure, there were the occasional hookups.

Single guys taking jobs here and there just to get by.

Men on the downlow who would never in a million years come out, but they made for a fun night in bed.

I made it a point to never hookup with guys who had family.

That just wasn't my thing.

My *thing* was tall, dark, and handsome.

And as much as I held our town and citizens dear to my heart, I longed for that perfect man to waltz into my life, sweep me off my feet, and devote the rest of his life to loving me and St. Nick's.

I snorted as I hefted my school bag onto my shoulder.

As if that would ever happen.

Yes, I believed in Christmas miracles—hell, I even believed in plain ol' miracles.

But a tall, dark, and handsome man strolling into St. Nicholas Crossing, falling in love with me and the town, *and* deciding to stay?

Far-fetched to say the least.

I wasn't saying it could never happen.

Wasn't saying I didn't *want* it to happen.

Just saying I wasn't holding my breath.

With a final wave to Candy and Ginger, I headed out of the school building. It wasn't large, but with only two-hundred-fifty students in any given year, it didn't need to be. We had one class per grade level and most of the middle and high school teachers taught multiple grades and subjects. While we weren't going to make the news for over-the-top academics or sports, our students gained a solid education and were ready for a job, the military, trade-school, or college when they graduated.

Walking along the holiday-decorated sidewalks on the icy-yet-sunshiny day, I took in St. Nicholas Crossing and recalled, yet again, that leaving this place just wasn't what my heart wanted—even though the fickle organ pumping in my chest wanted a lot of other things as well.

Jingle bells sounded throughout town for at least six weeks leading up to Christmas. Huge poinsettias adorned every house and shop front window from one end of town to the other. Cheery holiday flags hung from every light pole and seasonal songs played from speakers all over town.

Even when Christmas was over, the town maintained its holiday spirit and fun with a neighborhood named Vixen Village and street names such as Blitzen Boulevard, Prancer Parkway, Comet Circle, Cupid Court, Rudolph Road, Dancer Drive, Donner Drive, and Dasher Drive. Folks around town laughed that the original town planners got bored and dumped their creativity with those last three.

Continuing my walk to The Heart of St. Nicholas, I took a deep breath and enjoyed the unique scents. I'd never been able to explain it, but the time leading up to Christmas always had the town smelling of cinnamon, pine, chocolate, and peppermint. I'd given up trying to figure out how the glorious scent seemed to hang over our streets stirring up nostalgia and holiday cheer for over a month.

After the new year, the scent disappeared along with the jingle bells, music, and most of the decorations—although the shops and houses *always* had their front windows adorned with a seasonal flower and the light poles were never left bare—but the cheerful, welcoming sense of community was present year-round.

Sure, we had our busybodies.

Yeah, the gossip mill chugged along more efficiently than the trains which passed through our little town every hour of the day and night.

And the thought of finding a man to fall in love with and settle down was daunting to say the least.

But I had my parents.

My students.

The townsfolk I considered friends.

All the good St. Nick's Heart did for the town.

I could live without love and romance.

Or at least that was what I told myself.

Walking into The Heart of St. Nick, I returned my dad's smile and friendly wave. Tucking my school bag behind the counter, I unbuttoned the sleeves of my dress shirt and rolled them up.

"What needs doing?" I asked.

"Best-dressed helper in the store," Dad said with a wink

as he wrapped an arm around Mom's waist. "But your momma is still the prettiest."

I removed my colorful scarf—only one of the fashionable accessories I was known for around town—and jacket, hanging them on the back of a chair. Snapping my suspenders and matching bowtie, I smiled at the happiness pouring from my parents.

A pang of longing pinched my gut.

I wanted that.

"I'll take the compliment." While my bright scarves were a necessary fashion choice during the cold months, my other accessories were more personal style than necessity. My matching bowties and suspenders were always good for getting smiles, and the kids around town had made a game of checking out my crazy socks. While the socks didn't usually *match* my other accessories—come on, that would be overkill—I usually did a good job of at least blending them. And I saved my craziest socks for days when I wore more subdued suspenders and bowties.

My scarves were pretty much year-round as well, but I opted for lighter ones to offset an outfit during the warmer months. During the winter season, my scarves were thick and warm, not just for looking good.

"We got a new load of coats and hats, some shoes and boots, and hit the jackpot on some toys," Mom said, pointing toward the back of the store.

"Everything needs sorted through and organized," Dad said.

I clapped my hands together. "Perfect. I'll get started."

"In about two hours, Dad and I are heading to dinner with the Frosts. Could you cover the store until closing?" Mom asked.

"If you've got plans, we can ask Candy and Ginger to come help. They never mind."

I shook my head at my dad. "Plans? What are those?"

"You know," Mom started, "the things twenty-seven-year-old men often have with friends or partners?"

I waved her off. "You two have a great dinner. I'll have everything sorted and organized before I leave—or at least a good start on it—and we can start putting the new items out for the shoppers as soon as Monday."

The afternoon was interrupted by the shrill sound of a passing train.

Several trains went through on one of the four rails each day. Some went through in a roaring blur. Others found themselves stopped to unload or take on new loads. While a decent handful were paused in their journey for maintenance or repair.

But the clanging of the crossing bells, the shudder of engines and slam of metal, and the shrill warning horn never ceased. For those of us local to St. Nicholas Crossing, the sounds were as natural as breathing and didn't even phase us.

For visitors, the trains took a bit to get used to.

The windows of the store rattled as the current train passed through.

Dad gave a wave. "Well, then. We'll let you get to it. We'll holler when we're heading out."

The Heart of St. Nick wasn't only the hub of our tiny town, it was also how many of our families made ends meet and provided their children with a bit of happiness.

Joseph Snow, bless him, had been a life-long resident of St. Nicholas Crossing. His wife died giving birth to their son. That son left the area before he'd even turned eighteen—or that's the story most townsfolk knew—and left his father alone.

Joseph found out several years later he had a grandchild. The grandson, Gannon Snow, visited as a child often—most likely when his parents wanted to jet off on a vacation across the globe without their child in tow.

I recalled Gannon Snow coming to St. Nicholas Crossing when he was a teen—I would have been about ten years younger than him. The last time I saw the guy—during his very brief visit with his grandfather—I'd already realized girls weren't my thing and the image of sexy, aloof, worldly Gannon Snow had fueled my jerk-off sessions for years to come.

Anyway, back before his son took off, Joseph Snow set up The Heart of St. Nicholas as a way to give back—he'd not only come from money, he'd also made millions in his lifetime, although no one really knew details or understood why he was so drawn to the little town—and to provide for the struggling families, especially those with kids.

So, the little general store was expanded to house donated goods. The donations came from far and wide—although no one was ever one hundred percent sure where all of the donations came from as some huge loads would just occasionally show up with no identifying information. Toys, clothing, food, diapers, and money—which we used to buy stock that ran low—were the top needs and the things we still got the most of.

Once a month, on a rotation, each child was given the opportunity to shop for a book and a toy. Accompanying parents could pick out underwear, socks, a shirt, and pants for the child. Shoes were every six months to a year depending on our stock. School supplies were available for free before the year started and at Christmas time to help replenish what the child had at school—this was a huge help to the teachers as well.

As a birthday gift, each child under eighteen could come in and pick a toy or book within a week of their birthday.

We also provided toiletries, dry goods, tools, utensils,

shelf-stable meals, and more. Many of the parents were also able to take advantage of the shopping program by picking out work clothes, shoes, undergarments, and books.

Not every family needed the assistance.

Some took only what they needed when they needed it.

Some were in constant need.

There was nothing like watching the youngest children up to moody teens get toys, books, clothes, and toiletries they not only *needed* but also wanted.

The grateful appreciation from families and the smiles on young faces were the reasons why I cheerfully rolled up my sleeves and set to work sorting through the donations, checking our inventory, and organizing the new supplies for the next round of shopping.

While we sometimes got gently-used donations, we also received brand-new materials more often than not. We put each and every item to good use, but preferred to keep the brand-new materials for the kids' shopping days if possible.

It took a lot of organization and planning, but it was definitely worth it in the end.

Joseph's desire to provide for the families of St. Nicholas Crossing had grown into something big during his lifetime and the town had promised, upon his recent death, to keep his legacy alive with The Heart of St. Nick.

Keeping the store going wasn't without its challenges, and Joseph had provided us a timeline to prove we could make it work, but my family and the town had no intentions of letting St. Nick's Heart go under. Not only because so many benefitted from it, but because it warmed our hearts to know we were giving back to our community in such a needed way.

"So many toys," Mom said happily as she joined me at the loading dock.

"Only one of the pallets has any information on it. Came

from a large private school who ran a toy drive. The other ones are mysteries." I checked off some inventory on my clipboard.

"As usual, it seems," Mom said with a shrug. "Maybe they want to stay anonymous. Maybe they don't think about providing a name." She winked. "Maybe it's the good ol' Christmas magic running through this town that keeps the donations coming in year after year."

"Gotta love the Christmas magic," I said, picking up one of the new toys and smiling at the thought of a child opening it on Christmas Day.

The next round of shopping was a bit different.

Children would still get their pick of toy and book, but all of the biggest and best items would be put aside for parents or the oldest siblings to pick out Christmas gifts for the little ones. St. Nick's Heart never cared if the gifts were being presented as from Santa or from the family, we just loved the fact children weren't missing out on the season.

The children also got in on the giving. They were invited to come in and shop for their parents and siblings so they'd have gifts to give on Christmas Day as well.

The store gave away a lot, but it was well worth it.

And just about every family spent their hard-earned money at St. Nick's Heart when they needed groceries, toiletries, clothing, and such outside of the free shopping days—many really didn't have the means to travel to nearby towns for shopping and relied completely on our little store.

The Ginger Snap Café and Candy Cane Counter were attached to The Heart of St. Nick—owned by our very own Ginger and Candy, although they usually had younger folks running the places for them these days—and offered homecooked meals and homemade candies for decent prices.

I remembered a visitor asking Ginger and Candy once

why they put so much work into their meals and candies only to sell them so cheap.

The women had just smiled serenely and answered, "Who out there doesn't enjoy savoring a sweet or eating a good meal they didn't have to cook after a long day at work? Just because our town isn't wealthy doesn't mean we don't all deserve the same treats as others."

Often times, when The Heart got donations, there'd be a note with money saying to use it to cover a check at Ginger Snap Café or to offer a random gift certificate to a family who would most appreciate a free meal out.

Sometimes, we just earmarked extra funds for exactly that as well.

"Well, Dad and I are going to head out. Are you good to finish up here?" Mom asked.

"Yeah, I'll work for a bit longer and then head home."

I had the garage apartment at my parents' place. It was mostly private, plenty of room, and free—so the place was actually perfect for me.

"Are you planning any trips to the city anytime soon?" Mom asked, concern etched on her face.

Smiling softly, I shook my head. "Nah, gave that a try a couple times. Just didn't work out for me, ya know?" She was referring to the few times over the past years when I'd gone into the city to meet up with a date in hopes of striking up a spark.

But every failed date had just brought me down and I'd realized it just wasn't worth my time. I didn't like going into the city enough to put up with the letdown each blah date brought me.

I'd stick to the once or twice a year hook-ups I got in St. Nicholas Crossing and ask Santa to send me a tall, dark, and handsome man who loved me and wanted to spend the rest of his life in a poor, sleepy little railroad town helping me run a general store.

As if.

Mom frowned. "Well, I can't say I'm sorry to hear that. I didn't like you going there to meet with strangers."

Oh god, what would she think about the blowjobs I'd given in the dark shadows of the railyard? Or the times I'd snuck home after doing the walk of shame from the tiny houses down by the tracks when I'd spent hot, sweaty nights with men just traveling through?

"You can rest easy," I said.

"Dad and I do want you to meet someone and be happy," she started.

"Mom, I am happy. If a guy comes along, great. If not, I don't need a man in my life to complete me. I love my life and I love what I'm doing." The words were one hundred percent true, even if they stung my romantic, hopeful little homo heart.

She sighed and nodded. "Okay, well…"

"Enjoy your dinner with the Frosts."

Mom gave me a hug and I returned to my work, happily humming holiday tunes as I sorted toys sure to bring extreme joy to a lot of kids.

I hadn't been lying.

I *did* love my life.

And if I stayed busy and cheery enough to distract my heart from the one thing it didn't have, all the better.

CHAPTER 3
Gannon

ADMITTEDLY, the shiny sports car I'd rented at the airport was likely a poor choice for driving to St. Nicholas Crossing. While the railroad the town relied on wasn't *in* the hills—more at the base of them—much of the town was nestled in and around the hilly area and snow, altitude, and a sports car weren't a good combination.

But the car drove like a dream and I'd enjoyed the two-hour drive from the airport.

Enjoyed it right until I had to fight the car to make it up the first hill to St. Nicholas Crossing.

Then I realized I looked like a man in the middle of an early mid-life crisis trying to prove how big my dick was with a souped-up, shiny red sports car that probably cost more than two houses in the little railroad town.

There was no way the car would make it to my grandpa's place, so I eased the beauty into a spot near a park and killed the engine.

With a sigh, I glanced around.

Didn't look like much had changed.

God, how I'd loved the place as a kid.

Ridiculous to think back on it now, but St. Nicholas Crossing had been a haven for me.

Escape from my parents' fighting and taking it out on me.

Time with my grandfather.

Holiday cheer.

Streets named after reindeer.

I'd looked forward to my visits year after year.

Until I didn't.

My heart pinched, guilt coursing through my veins.

What had made me stop coming?

Being jaded by my parents. Their toxic relationship and combination of verbal abuse and neglect of me did a number on my head and heart.

Focusing more on money and success than on family. Money and success didn't lash out or make you feel bad. I'd found them and they were a lot easier to deal with than some of the people in my life.

And the little trick I'd learned of walling myself off from people emotionally so as not to have to *do* the whole getting-my-heart-involved thing. I knew I had issues with getting too close to people. It didn't take a rocket scientist to figure that out. It wasn't even a challenge to figure out *why* I was leery of relationships.

It's not that I didn't want a happy, healthy, loving relationship with a man.

I just didn't want to watch it die a slow, painful death like my parents' marriage and ruin the lives of those around me.

So, money and success were my focus.

And now your grandfather is dead and you have no one.

Gut churning, I climbed out of the car.

I didn't often allow myself to think about Grandpa and how good he'd been to me, but when I did, I suffocated in heavy guilt.

I should have been there for him.

Should have set aside my stubborn pride and at least let *him* in.

It was a lot easier to hunker down behind my walls than to deal with people-y entanglements.

But he was my grandfather, for god's sake.

What did Joseph Snow think as he watched his only grandson, child of his estranged and now deceased son, inch further and further away with each passing year?

I stayed away to keep up the walls.

The walls kept my heart safe.

But they also cost me my only family.

And now he was gone.

The guilt and pain trying to swallow me whole battled with the good memories of the little town. I wanted to replace the bad with the good, but I wasn't sure I had it in me.

No.

I was here for a purpose.

God rest his soul, Grandpa had left his house and store to me.

I'd get it in sale-ready condition and work as quickly as I could to sell.

Then I was out.

Where do you really need to be? You could stay for a while. Reconnect with him if only through stories and memories.

The thought punched me in the gut.

When was the last time you were truly happy and content? This place has always had a hold on your heart if you'd just let go.

No, it was best if I swooped in, did my job, and left as quickly as I'd arrived.

True, nothing was holding me to LA.

I could work from anywhere. Hell, I knew Ellen would be willing to keep up with her duties through virtual meetings.

But with Grandpa gone, nothing tied me to St. Nicholas Crossing either.

I had no connections in the town other than fond recollections of far-off times with my grandfather.

What good would those do me?

Gathering my scattered thoughts and stomping down my wishy-washy heart, I locked the car and pocketed the key. I'd need a lift to my grandpa's house up the hill and I hoped I'd find a cooperative and easy-going person to assist in giving me a ride at The Heart of St. Nick, the little general store my grandfather had owned.

Challenging myself to be in and out of town in under a week—yeah, it was a stretch, but it would keep me on a schedule and not give me time to get caught up in the place —I breathed deeply as if steeling myself against the emotions this place had stirred. The scent of cinnamon, chocolate, pine, and peppermint gently assaulted my senses, reminding me of years gone by and the comforts this damn town always brought me.

And obviously still brings you.

"Welcome to The Heart of Saint Nick," a cheery voice called from somewhere in the little store as jingle bells chimed over the door to announce my arrival.

Little store was a misnomer.

The place had grown a lot since my last visit.

"Feel free to look around," the happy helper said. "I'll be right with you."

Trying to contain my eye roll at the peppy person I already knew would be over-the-top in the holiday spirit, I wandered the store.

When I was younger, the place had seemed huge. But now, it truly was quite large. Instead of the small counter of snacks and desserts I remembered, there was now a full-blown café and candy store. Ginger Snap Café and Candy Cane Counter weren't the only additions to The Heart.

Walls had been knocked down to add on space and there seemed to be much more going on than just the little grocery and toiletries area I remembered.

Toys, clothes, shoes, and school supplies lined several aisles adjacent to the groceries and toiletries. As I gazed around the place, I took in the fact there appeared to be two distinct sections.

One side had signs with prices.

One side had signs with number limits.

Frowning, I made note to ask about that if and when the damn cheerful little voice ever made itself known.

"Sorry about that."

Startled, I jerked to a stop.

"Oops, didn't mean to scare you."

I turned around only to be punched right in the gut.

The cheery voice belonged to the most beautiful man I'd ever seen—as far away from *my type* as one could get, but gorgeous all the same.

Russet-colored hair straddling the line between stylishly messy and just plain out of control, pale skin with warm undertones and the slightest hint of freckles, dark grayish-blue eyes, and the most deliciously-kissable mouth I'd ever seen.

"Hi, I'm Hayden Green. You're not a regular. Just passing through or here for a visit?" He stuck out his hand with a cheery, genuine smile as he stood there looking ridiculously cute in a matching bowtie and suspenders in a snowman print.

The hot jolt of awareness and desire that smacked me when I took his hand had me wondering if I'd somehow landed in a cheesy Hallmark-ish type holiday romance. His skin was soft and warm against mine and I wanted to yank him close, wrap him in my arms, and forget everything, even if just for the night.

Forcing the thoughts away, I let go of his hand and cleared my throat. "Gannon Snow."

Hayden's eyes widened, but he recovered quickly. "Welcome back to The Crossing, Mr. Snow. Terribly sorry about your grandfather's passing."

"Thank you. I need to get up to Joseph's place and start organizing and packing." I gestured toward the general vicinity of Grandpa's house and my useless-on-icy-roads car. "Any chance I could get a ride up the hill?"

Hayden wrinkled his nose. "Sorry to say, but no-can-do."

"I can pay you," I said.

Hayden smiled. "No need for that. I'd gladly take you up to Joseph's place, but there's a big ol' tree down. Crew showed up today to start clearing it, but it's a monster and is going to take a day or so before they get the road opened up again."

Pinching the bridge of my nose, I sighed. "What are people up on the hill supposed to do for a couple days?"

Hayden shrugged. "Same as they do when it gets too icy or a foot of snow falls. Wait it out. They've all got emergency supplies. Probably thinkin' they're damn lucky it's just a tree and not an ice storm—at least they've still got power and Wi-Fi."

"They've got Wi-Fi up there?" I asked, my brow scrunching as I recalled my last stay at Grandpa's as a teen. Of course, technology back then hadn't been what it was today, but to hear they'd gotten Wi-Fi up the hill was hard to wrap my head around. Hell, I was impressed they'd even gotten a good signal in town.

Hayden grinned. "Sure do. Saint Nick's is sitting pretty where technology is concerned. An anonymous donor started providing Wi-Fi a long time ago—it's free and probably better than what a lot of people in the city can get."

With my head still stuck on the last time I stayed at Grandpa's, I frowned. "Wi-Fi is great," I said, selfishly glad I'd be able to work and stay connected. "But what do people use it for?"

Hayden chuckled and shook his head. "We're not as backward as you might think, Mr. Snow. A grant from the state provides each child a device for school. My mom is a grant-writing-queen and she received another chunk of money that provides each home with a device—mostly laptops. We've got a deal with a phone store a couple towns over where they offer trades on gently-used phones and tablets. Our residents may never have brand new phones or tablets, but they usually get ones that are only a year or so old. They're nice, they're free, and they work so it's a win."

I found myself wanting to listen to Hayden talk all day, but that was dangerous territory—and also very confusing because conversation wasn't my usual go-to and Hayden wasn't even close to the type of guy I'd ever even consider hooking up with. Too cheery, too real, too small-town.

"Well, I'll need a room then. Does the little motel still exist?" I asked, ready to move the conversation along so I could stop thinking about how bitable his plump pink bottom lip was.

Hayden winced. "Sure does. Exist that is. But it's all full up with the tree-cutting crew."

Trying to breathe through the frustration, I closed my eyes and rubbed a knuckle over the frown lines between my brows. "Of course it is."

I couldn't sleep in my damn car.

Well, I *could* have if I hadn't splurged on the ridiculous sports car.

Truly, there was no room to sleep in that sleek red beauty.

"I have a spare room you're welcome to," Hayden said.

"That won't be necessary," I started.

He shrugged. "Me offering may not be necessary, but unless you're sleeping in your car or outside, the room actually *is* necessary. Come on, we'll get you settled in. We can take in the town tomorrow—you can do whatever important big-city work you need to do—and hopefully on the day after the tree will be cleared and I can get you up the hill to Joseph's place."

Fighting the urge to argue—I really didn't do well when things didn't go as planned—I sighed. "Yeah, okay. Thanks."

"Let me just wrap a couple things up and then I'll be good to go." Hayden headed to a little back room, leaving me alone in the middle of the store.

What was back there?

Hell, the store was pretty much mine, I had every right to go check it out.

Right?

Deciding to cover up my curiosity, I moved toward where he'd disappeared to and asked, "Anything I can do to help?"

"That's super sweet of you, but I've got it almost all taken care of." Hayden gestured towards boxes and organized piles, shelves, racks, and stacks.

"Wow, what's all this?"

He grinned and I suddenly thought making him smile should be my main goal in life.

Don't be stupid. You're here a week. He's at least ten years younger than you. He isn't even close to the type of guy you're attracted to. Plus, you don't even know if he's gay.

I covered my snort with a soft cough. I'd seen the man's snowmen bowtie and the matching suspenders—the latter completely just for looks because those well-fitting pants didn't need a single bit of help to stay up with that tight little bubble butt doing a masterful job all by itself. There was absolutely no doubt in my mind about the man's sexuality.

"This," Hayden said, sweeping his arm to the room, "is what we do."

"Organize items?"

He chuckled. "Yes, but no. We get donations from all over the state and the country—money, food, needed items, clothing—and we make sure it's ready for our monthly shoppers in need."

"Monthly shoppers?"

"Yeah, every kid in town gets to come pick out a toy and a book. Their parents can pick clothing for them. Parents get to gather work clothes and toiletries for themselves. We also do school supplies." He threw a fond glance over the donations he'd been organizing. "But *these* are being saved for Christmas shopping. The Heart of Saint Nick makes it our mission to be sure our families, especially the kids, have a Christmas full of love." He pointed a finger at me. "And it's all because of Joseph Snow."

My stomach sank.

Did Hayden not know I was here to sell the store?

Why would he think the town would just get to keep my grandfather's property?

Probably best if I got a place to sleep and a ride up the hill before he found out St. Nick's Heart belonged to me and I was definitely selling.

You're really going to take away a store your grandpa started? A place that provides kids and families with needs and wants?

I huffed.

It wasn't anything personal.

Not at all.

It was business only.

Sell the house.

Sell the store.

Leave St. Nicholas Crossing and never look back.

Ha. Never look back like you did all those years ago when you left the best person you've ever known all alone?

It wasn't as if Joseph had been alone.

Clearly, he'd had the town.

And the store.

And helping folks.

But I wasn't here to continue in his footsteps.

Hell, I was a real estate agent, not a philanthropist.

Selling was a must.

The money would be used to finalize any of Grandpa's outstanding debts and then likely be put away to earn interest and grow.

Maybe I'd even donate some to the town.

Yeah, that's what I'd do.

Donate a large chunk from the sale to the town in Joseph's name.

"Your grandpa was the absolute epitome of a giving Christmas spirit."

"He was a good guy," I mumbled, my words totally inadequate.

Hayden wrapped a colorful scarf around his neck and shrugged into a winter coat. "Okay, I'll let you drive to my place since I walked here from school." He slung a leather bag over his shoulder.

"School?" Oh god, was I lusting over an under-aged kid?

He grinned. "I'm a teacher. Part time English. And part time here at the store."

Hayden locked the front door and gestured for me to follow him out the back.

"Which way is your car?"

"Oh, um, at the park."

I took in the poinsettias in all the front windows and the holiday themed flags hanging from light poles as we walked from Cupid Court to Prancer Parkway. The damn little Christmas town was even more over-the-top than I remembered it. And the holiday music being piped from speakers on every corner only proved my point.

"Whoa, is that yours?" Hayden whistled as we approached the parking lot next to the park.

"Rental. Not the smartest move in hindsight." I unlocked the car and popped the tiny trunk for Hayden to shove in his bag. "Not exactly good on ice and my bags barely fit."

"Sure is pretty though," Hayden said as he slid into the car.

Suddenly bombarded with images of him in a convertible, sunshine on his face, wind whipping his hair as we drove down the Pacific highway, I cleared my throat and did what I did best.

Got grumpy to block out emotions at all costs.

"Don't you ever get tired of the Christmas music? Decorations? *Everything?*" I asked, slamming my door and revving the engine to life.

Hayden blinked innocently as he studied my face. "Not at all. I love it. I can't imagine living anywhere that doesn't celebrate the magic of Christmas—but more than that, it's just the cheerful, giving spirit of this place. It's comforting."

I harrumphed. "Well, I'm not here for the holiday displays or magic or whatever you're selling. I'm here to take care of my grandfather's estate and get back to LA."

"Ah," Hayden hummed, "the part of the grumpy visitor will now be played by Gannon Snow. Gotcha."

"What?" I asked, whipping my head toward him.

Hayden shrugged. "If we were in a movie or stage production, I'd be the cheerful, friendly townie and you'd be the grumpy visitor swooping in. We'd be forced to work together for the greater good despite you being here for nefarious reasons. We'd both learn about ourselves and grow into better people by the end of the story."

I snorted. "Well, good thing this is real life then."

"No nefarious reasons?" Hayden asked, cocking his pretty head.

Pretending to be focused on a sharp turn, I ignored the question. "You've really never wanted to live anywhere else?"

Hayden narrowed his eyes, but took the distraction. "I went to college and truly thought I'd stay gone. But the city wasn't for me. This place has my heart. I'm old enough now to realize this is where I belong. Kinda like you belong in the city?"

I shrugged with a grunt. "Something like that," I mused. "How old are you?"

He looked about twenty-three, but I'd bet he was older.

"Twenty-seven. Not past my prime by any means, but I've been around long enough to know this is where I want to be. I like to stay busy and help people."

Glancing his way, I waited for him to continue—almost like I *knew* he had more to say.

Hayden shrugged. "Even though I love this place and wouldn't go anywhere else, it gets lonely. Staying busy helps and helping people makes it worth it."

"But the loneliness never really goes away," I muttered mostly to myself.

Damn.

I definitely knew that feeling.

"What?"

"Nothing." I glanced out the window. "Things haven't really changed much around here since the last time I was here."

Hayden grinned. "Last time you were here, I was just a kid and I thought the cute, older guy visiting from the city was the coolest thing I'd ever seen. I wanted to go off to

California just like Joseph Snow's grandson and do something big." He chuckled. "Instead, I went a couple hours away, got my degree, tried to make it work in the city, and never felt truly content until I made my way back here to stay."

"And now you are? Truly content?"

He pointed to a driveway within the cozy little neighborhood of Vixen Village and gave a rueful laugh. "I'm in a perpetual Christmas town helping folks in need alongside my parents whom I adore."

"Ah, the part of the evasively cheerful townsperson will now be played by Hayden Green," I deadpanned.

Hayden threw his head back and laughed.

My breath caught in my throat.

He was the most beautiful man I'd ever seen.

Fuck.

I needed to take care of things and get the hell out of here.

Why not test the waters? See if he's down for a little fling while you're here. Could be fun.

My dick twitched behind my zipper.

He *had* said he'd thought I was cute way back then.

I didn't think a fling was the best idea, but I *was* leaving soon so *no-strings-attached* would be easy.

Maybe it wouldn't hurt to at least see if he was on board.

But he'd said he got lonely.

Was it fair to take advantage of that?

He's a big boy. He can make his own decisions on what's right and wrong. If you don't let him know you'd be interested in a quick fling, he'll never know. At least let him know so he can make the decision for himself.

And if I put myself out there and Hayden shot me down?

Not something I was fond of, but it wasn't as if I'd be around long enough to wallow in rejection.

"Here we are," Hayden said, completely changing the subject as if I wouldn't notice. "The big house is my parents'. They let me stay in the garage apartment. It's more room than I actually need since the garage is huge, but it's free and private." He directed me where to park my car under an overhang and we got out.

I grabbed my bags and followed him up the stairway on the side of the garage.

"Careful, there may be ice," Hayden warned. "I keep them cleared as much as possible—real bitch in the icy winter months—but sometimes they still get slick." He opened the door at the top of the stairs and held it for me as I walked past him.

"No locked doors?" I asked.

"Nah, it's pretty safe around here. I don't have a lot of valuables. While you're here, I'll keep everything locked up tight."

I wanted to protest and say it was no problem, but the idea of leaving the doors unlocked was a completely foreign concept to me. "Thanks."

"Here's the spare bedroom." Hayden gestured toward a little corner of the vast apartment. "*Room* is kinda a misnomer." He winced. "Sorry, it's not completely private, but the bed is real nice and the sheets are clean. Plenty of hot water for a shower. Towels are in the closet." He pointed to a door I assumed was the bathroom. "Wi-Fi password is sa1ntn1xb0y," he said, his ears red as he scribbled the mix of letters and numbers on a piece of paper. "Tomorrow, I'll show you around town if you'd like. We can eat here or at the Ginger Snap. You can hang out at the store or here if you have work to do."

"Sounds good."

A shrill train whistle filled the air.

"Damn, that's one sound I never really got used to when I'd visit. Doesn't it just grate on your nerves?"

Hayden shook his head with a smile. "Nah, barely even notice it. That's how you can tell the difference between a local and a visitor."

I huffed. "Not sure I'd ever be able to not notice *that*. Any chance you think they'll get the tree cleared earlier?" I asked as I threw my bags on the bed and toed off my shoes.

Hayden wrinkled his nose. "I doubt it, it truly was a beast of a tree. But if I hear it's clear, I'll be sure to let you know." He pointed to his bag. "I'm going to grade papers with some hot tea if you want to shower and settle in. You're welcome to work at the table. Do you want tea? Eggnog? Water?"

I winced. "Eggnog? Do people really drink that?"

Hayden laughed. "It's homemade and really good. I don't do the raw egg recipe and I only add brandy on days that have been really rough. Not a fan?"

I shook my head. "I tasted it once and almost gagged. It's not for me."

"Fair enough. I do have brandy if you'd like a drink. Or peppermint tea? It's decaf in case you're worried about sleeping."

"You really are the quintessential spirit-of-the-holidays guy aren't you?"

Hayden shrugged. "It's just who I am."

Caught off guard by the vulnerability in his eyes, I said, "It's not a bad thing. Just not something I'm used to. Warm welcomes and feeling wanted aren't really a thing where I'm from."

Hayden cocked his head with a sad smile. "That's too bad. Everyone should have a place where they feel welcome and wanted."

Had I ever had that?

You had it here with Joseph until you turned your back to focus more on money and success.

Guilt and longing pulled at my heart.

This place truly was the one and only location I'd ever felt welcome and wanted—loved even—and I'd gone and screwed that up by hiding my heart and letting my desire for money and success take over.

If I was being honest, it wasn't even the money and success I wanted—although, they were a nice byproduct—it was the ability to stay busy and detached, to close myself off while striving toward that money and success that I wanted most of all.

If I kept my heart closed, I didn't have to feel.

Didn't have to hurt.

Sure, it was cold and lonely, but keeping out *all* the feels protected me from the negative ones.

And, thanks to my parents, I'd realized long ago I wanted to protect myself from painful emotions.

I cleared my throat and grabbed some clothes and toothbrush from my bag. "I'm not the type to need warm welcomes and being wanted. I'll take some brandy, thanks." I made a beeline for what I hoped was the bathroom door and locked it quickly behind me.

Taking a piss and stripping naked, I tried to ignore the sound of Hayden singing holiday songs as he bustled about making his peppermint tea. After turning on the vent to drown out the singing, I found a towel in the closet. Holding it to my nose, I breathed in the soft scent of cinnamon and pine.

Why did the whole damn town smell like all the best memories of my past? Did they fog the place each season? Huge trucks with machines pumping holiday scents over the unsuspecting citizens?

Or, since it *was* St. Nicholas Crossing, maybe they had

little elves with those old-fashioned fire blowers—bellows?—
tiptoeing around town in the wee hours puffing magical,
mesmerizing scents into every nook and cranny.

Scents laden with something almost hypnotizing.

That had to be it.

I'd been in town only a few hours and already felt dazed
and discombobulated.

And I was imagining elves with bellows.

I was definitely out of sorts.

Shower first.

Brandy.

Some work.

And a good night's sleep.

That's what I needed.

I'd feel better in the morning.

Turning my attention back to the task at hand, I couldn't
help chuckling at the decorative holiday soaps brightening up
Hayden's sink—not that I was surprised, as I'd already seen
his festive tree in a corner of the apartment and plenty of
decorations. I wondered if he kept the décor up year-round or
switched it out with each passing holiday.

One thing was for sure, I needed to stop *wondering* about
Hayden at all.

Needing something to focus on other than the beautiful,
cheery man currently making hot tea on the other side of the
door, I turned on a playlist and increased the volume. I didn't
care what the songs were as long as they weren't Christmas
songs and I couldn't hear Hayden whistling his cheery tune.

Realizing I'd forgotten my toothpaste, I opened the
medicine cabinet.

A prescription bottle of PrEP stared back at me.

Slamming the door closed, I yanked open the drawer.

An enema kit sat there, mocking me.

Damn it all to hell, did the kid not have any toothpaste?

Ah, there it was.

Ignoring the irrefutable proof Hayden was gay or bi—and very likely bottomed at least some of the time—I violently brushed my teeth while trying to focus on the music filling the tiny bathroom.

Turning the shower temperature up as hot as I could stand, I climbed in and let the wet heat wash away the stress of travel and being off-kilter.

Shit.

Soap and shampoo.

I'd left both in my bag.

Grabbing Hayden's shampoo, I groaned as the scent of peppermint, balsam fir, and grapefruit filled the air.

Fuck.

This was what the kid smelled like.

Stop calling him a kid. He's a grown man and he's got your dick harder than it's been for anyone in years.

I scrubbed my hair and rinsed.

The bottle of body wash was the same scent and I cursed my damn erection as I washed myself.

Rinsing, I concluded I had two choices.

Submitting to an icy blast of cold water.

Or jerking off.

The latter option would benefit in relaxing me instead of keeping me tense and anxious, so I borrowed one last dollop of body wash and fisted my cock in my slick palm.

When I had the time, I enjoyed edging myself to completion.

But jerking off in a virtual stranger's shower was not the time for drawn-out and sensual.

I closed my eyes and gripped my shaft, stroking and twisting as I imagined an anonymous sweet, hot mouth sucking me off. A tight little hole stretching around me. Lean, muscular thighs straddling my hips and riding my dick.

And then Hayden's face intruded.

It was Hayden's pretty pink mouth stretched around my cock.

Hayden bent over for me, opening for my throbbing dick.

Straddling me and rolling his hips as he took my cock deep.

Fuck.

The orgasm crashed over me and I gritted my teeth to keep from groaning his name. My soft grunts were hopefully not audible over the vent and music, but I'd been reckless to let myself go with Hayden right in the other room.

What the hell was this town doing to me?

What was *Hayden* doing to me?

I didn't get all wrapped up in men. I didn't *do* angst or pining or fluttery swirly feelings.

Especially not with men I'd just met, and I'd be damned if I was going to start now.

Rinsing again before shutting off the water, I climbed out and dried with the fluffy, cinnamon and pine scented towel.

With my bones liquified and my body begging to slip under blankets and sleep off the best orgasm I'd had in—well, maybe in forever—I dressed quickly, ran the towel through my hair, and turned off my music before exiting the bathroom.

The cool air chilled my skin and I hung my clothes on the footboard of my borrowed bed—completely ignoring the fact I'd only moments earlier been jacking off to the image of fucking my host.

"Brandy," Hayden said, pointing to the tumbler on the table. "And I went ahead and made you peppermint tea, just in case."

This. Man.

He was like a little cheery helper bringing sunshine and goodness to all who knew him.

Hayden was dangerous.

His cute, cheery smile.

Those dark grayish-blue eyes.

His gentle, helpful spirit.

The way he just immediately took me in, treated me as if we'd known each other forever, and chipped away at my icy heart was *DAN-GER-OUS*.

Between the hypnotic-scent-cloud-of-holiday-goodness floating over the town, music that probably sent subliminal messages to a person's brain, memories of Grandpa, and now Hayden looking so fucking cute and being so damn sweet...

Yeah, I needed to get out of town.

Stat.

Like ASAP.

"Thanks," I muttered, quickly swallowing the finger of brandy he'd poured for me.

Hayden's eyes widened. "Want another? You know, maybe to *sip*?"

Breathing through the burn, I nodded, ignoring his cute little smirk. "Please."

Determined to savor the liquor, I walked to the bed, grabbed my laptop from my bag, and returned to the table. Maybe keeping my distance was safer, but I was a grown-ass, professional man. I could sit at the damn kitchen table with a cute, sexy guy and not get turned on.

Because you just shot your load down his bathtub drain. Give it thirty minutes.

Fuck.

I saved the brandy for later and sipped the peppermint tea —only wondering for a brief moment if it was laced with some sort of holiday magic potion—and we settled in to work on our individual projects.

About an hour later, Hayden groaned. "Oh my god, these papers about killed me."

"That bad, huh?" Damn it. I should have just grunted a reply and stayed focused on my work. But I wasn't truly working, just trying to look busy as I attempted to figure out how in the hell I felt so damn at-ease in this stranger's garage apartment.

I hadn't felt so good in years.

So comfortable.

So calm.

I refused to believe in holiday magic or Christmas spirit or whatever Hayden and the town might preach.

What else could it be? You've been in LA for years and never felt this way. A couple hours in this quaint little town and all of a sudden you're all zen and having trouble blocking out his pretty eyes and sweet smile.

Fuck.

"Not *bad*," Hayden said, stretching with a moan that went straight to my dick. "Just long and not all of them caught on to the gist of the assignment, so I've got reteaching to do."

"But you like your job overall?"

Hayden grinned. "I do. Sometimes, I think I'd like to teach full-time, but that would take me away from The Heart."

"Wouldn't teaching be better money than a tiny general store?" A zing of guilt shot through me at the thought I'd be costing some people their jobs.

"Oh, I don't get paid at the store," Hayden said. "The part-time teaching pay isn't great, but cost of living is super low around here." He gestured around his apartment. "I'm lucky my parents let me live here rent-free, I wouldn't be able to swing it on the part-time salary."

"How many people work at the store?"

Maybe if someone in town bought it—or even someone from the city—they'd keep the locals on as employees.

That could work, right?

Anything to get your money and ease your guilt, huh?

"Mom and Dad, but they don't take huge salaries—they basically get paid a small base and then they only get paid more if the store is doing well. So, they're definitely determined to make sure the store is successful, even beyond making sure people get what they need." Hayden smiled and sipped his tea. "There are two other older employees who work part-time to offset their pensions, a couple high schoolers who work to save money for college, and then Ginger and Candy, plus their little crews at the café and candy shop."

Shit.

This was why detached, aloof, and stoic served me well in real-estate. If I didn't get to know the place, the people, the story, it was a lot easier to just go in, sell, and leave.

But I didn't even know these people and I already felt like a monster.

"Are there a lot of job opportunities in town?" I asked, wincing as yet another train traveled by, its shrill whistle announcing its presence.

Hayden raised a brow. "We're a small railroad town nestled in the hills. The nearest big city is two hours away. If a person doesn't work at the school, the store, or the railroad, they *may* have a chance as a barber or hairstylist— maybe doing clothing alterations—or mechanic work. But we've got a barber and hairstylist for the time being. Most everyone around here can work on their own vehicles. And clothing alterations in a poor town doesn't earn a whole lot."

"What do most folks do?"

Hayden shrugged. "Most are here because of the railroad. It's hard work, but it pays and it's steady. If they don't work at the school or the store, some will do online work of some sort." His eyes twinkled. "I'm pretty sure there are at least a handful of single folks and couples doing sexy videos for online sites."

My face must have betrayed my thoughts because Hayden laughed.

"Not *me*," he said. "That wouldn't be good for my teaching career. Plus, who would pay to see me strip and jerk off?"

He asked it like the answer was *no one*, but damn if my dick didn't strain in my pants with a *Me, me, me!*

Watching him jerk off in just those suspenders and bowtie?

Take. My. Money.

Pushing the scorching hot image from my mind, I grasped for something. Anything. "No girlfriend to make videos with?" Okay, that was pathetic and lame, but the masochistic part of my brain needed to know for sure.

Hayden's ears pinked as he snapped his suspenders and straightened his bowtie. "In addition to being all about decking the halls and donning my gay apparel, I enjoy the company of the Mr. Clauses over the Ms. Clauses."

Time stood still as I blinked slowly, sifting through his words.

Mostly because I'd gotten my answer in his cute little confession.

Partly because I didn't know how someone could so effortlessly slot all-things-holiday into conversations.

"I'm gay," Hayden supplied helpfully when I hadn't replied.

Clearing my throat, I shifted in my seat. "Yeah, got that."

"And you?"

"What?"

"I didn't want to assume," Hayden said, a flush filling his cheeks. "Joseph once mentioned something about just wanting you happy with whichever man stole your heart…"

"No one's stolen my heart," I bit out, covering up the pang in my heart at the thought of Joseph wanting that for me *and* how much Hayden's hopeful eyes made me want things I shouldn't even be thinking about, much less wanting.

Damn, things I shouldn't even be actually considering.

What about that chance for a fling? You've confirmed he's gay. You're definitely into him. Why not have some fun on your trip?

Hayden's face had fallen with my little proclamation, but he soldiered on cheerfully. "So, moving back to jobs, if they don't work here, there's a decent number who drive trucks hauling loads either within the state or cross-country. Then there are people who drive a bit to some of the other small towns around here for jobs. A few people go into the city and stay in cheap hotels while they work the week before driving back on weekends."

I frowned. "Why not just live in the city?"

Hayden snorted. "Cost of living? Not to mention, most of us who live here would be leaving our hearts if we tried to live anywhere else. Believe me, I know. The place may give *you* hives, but we love it here."

I couldn't help the chuckle escaping my lips. "Maybe not hives exactly…"

Hayden cocked a brow.

"I'm just not used to it. It's very different from LA. I have good memories of this place." And while I found myself longing for the detached, aloof anonymity of the big city, I also couldn't dispel the fact my postage-stamp-sized heart was valiantly fighting—and currently losing—to stay frozen under the assault of the heartwarming holiday town.

And the man sitting across the table from me wasn't helping in the least.

Damn, man, you've only been here half a day. What's gonna happen by the end of your self-proclaimed one-week deadline?

Ignoring my stupid head, and hoping to protect my emotions, I quickly swallowed the rest of my brandy. "Well, I've done about all the work I can do for the night. I'm going to head to bed."

Hayden blinked rapidly at the quick-change in conversation, but nodded. "Good night. I'm going to shower first, but I'll try to keep quiet."

"No worries, I'm a pretty deep sleeper."

After packing up my bag, I climbed into bed.

The quietness of the night was deafening compared to LA, so I was grateful for Hayden's puttering around and showering.

Then there was the damn train.

It made my ears want to bleed in protest. So loud, so shrill, so distracting.

As if conjured from thin air, the train whistle sounded in the distance.

It would get louder and louder as the train got closer and closer.

At least we weren't *right* by the tracks. Windows shook and you felt the train vibrations to your bones. Those who lived near the tracks not only dealt with the whistle, but with the constant screeching of brakes, clanging of bells, and crashing of metal as the cars were switched and swapped.

Because of the importance of the railroad to St. Nicholas Crossing, Grandpa had made sure I'd understood how the processes worked. He'd taught me to respect the business even if I didn't like it or see myself ever involved with it.

But he'd never been able to get me used to the damn shrieking train whistle.

Smiling in the dark, I recalled Joseph telling me I'd learn to ignore it, possibly even take comfort in it, if I ever stayed longer.

As a child, all I wanted to do was stay forever.

As a teen, the itch to spread my wings began.

And now?

Beyond my understanding, I was torn.

Not that I'd give any *real* thought to staying in St. Nicholas Crossing any longer than was necessary. There was nothing for me in this place except memories.

But from the moment I'd driven into town, a tiny finger of *something* had been poking at me, trying to get me to…get me to what? I wasn't exactly sure.

Stay?

Admit how much this place and my grandfather meant to me?

Open myself up?

Was it the nostalgia? The ridiculous *magic* of the town—which I did *not* believe in—attempting to weasel its way into my mind? Or maybe Hayden's hospitality and warm smile?

Or maybe you're just in desperate need of a sweet, sexy ass and his has you all kinds of fucked up.

Huffing, I rolled to my side and yanked the blankets up over my head.

Luckily, the next day would give me a bit of a reprieve from Hayden's pretty pink lips and cute little bubble butt. When he went to the store, I'd stay at his place to work. If he invited me for lunch, I'd claim to be too busy.

I needed to avoid him.

He was too cute—and again, what the hell was that? Not. My. Type.

He was also too nice.

I needed to remember I was in town for one thing and one thing only.

Sell the house and the store.

Hayden would be crushed and I didn't need any kind of entanglement between us when he figured out what was going on.

So, why not tell him now?

A weird prickly feeling filled my chest at the thought. I knew I should. Should tell him exactly what my plans were.

But...

Mmhm. You're being selfish. Might as well take advantage of his hospitality before you piss him off, right? Maybe work your way into his pants first?

Hating the confusing mixture of thoughts swirling in my head—just proof of why keeping people at arm's length and not allowing emotions to get involved was always for the best —I focused on my breathing and the sound of the shower running.

I wouldn't think about selling the store and stealing people's jobs.

I wouldn't think about the weird little stabby feeling in my heart telling me I needed this damn little town.

I wouldn't think about whatever manufactured magic—or *natural* magic, even though none of that shit actually existed —the town was pumping out to keep its visitors and residents dazed and confused.

And I most definitely wouldn't think about Hayden Green.

The sparkle in his almost navy-gray eyes.

The pink of his lips—and how good they'd look opening for my dick.

What he'd look like riding my cock.

If the flush of his cheeks traveled to other places on his body.

The stretch of my lips around his shaft.

How badly I wanted to spread him open for my tongue and cock.

No.

I wouldn't think of those things.

The next day, I'd call Ellen and check in—not that she needed checking on, but it would give me something to do.

I'd work.

I'd stay focused.

And I'd be one day closer to getting the fuck out of this mesmerizing little Christmas town once and for all.

CHAPTER 4

Hayden

AFTER A LONG SHOWER—AND jerking off until my eyes rolled back in my head while I tried *not* to imagine dropping to my knees for Gannon Snow—I'd climbed into bed and fallen asleep taking comfort in the train horn blasting and listening to my guest toss and turn for at least an hour.

Sometime during the night, I woke to the distinct sound of ice against the windows. In the back of my mind, I chalked up the next day to a wash and hoped the ice would melt quickly if the sun showed its face.

Gannon and I could work from home.

No problem.

None at all.

I could totally sip eggnog all day and work on lesson plans. My students would do virtual learning. I could make notes on things needing done at the store. And I'd watch the video of the children's holiday pageant to see what parts needed revised and tightened up.

It would be a good work day.

A chance to catch up.

Maybe even watch a movie or bake cookies.

All while the sexiest man I'd ever seen sat brooding in my kitchen.

From the first moment Gannon walked through the door of The Heart, I'd known something was—different? Special? Off? I couldn't put a finger on it, but something was in the air.

I'd also known he was hot.

Hot as hell.

Hot as sin.

Sex on legs.

A walking wet dream.

You name it, Gannon was it.

I'd thought he was gorgeous, sophisticated, and mysterious way back when I'd last seen him.

Now, though?

Less mysterious and more aloof—detached—like he didn't want to get too close.

Maybe not so much sophisticated, but he'd grown accustomed to big-city living versus small-town life.

Definitely still gorgeous.

Slightly taller than my six feet.

Just enough scruff to make me want to feel it rough against my skin.

Lips I longed to savor.

Intense blue eyes.

And I swore Gannon looked at me with interest.

Maybe it was wishful thinking on my part, but I'd definitely caught him staring a time or two.

We'd established we were both gay. How reckless would it be to consider a fling while he was in town?

I usually stuck to one-time-only sex because my heart always wanted to get too involved when anything lasted longer than one-n-done.

But Gannon wasn't staying.

Not that I wouldn't want him to, but he was an LA guy. No way he'd want to stick around St. Nicholas Crossing to run a tiny store in the frigid cold. Yeah, he'd maybe like the summers better, but Gannon had better things to do.

However, if I knew going in that he would be gone soon, maybe I could just enjoy what I knew would be the best sex of my life and let him leave with my pockets full of amazing memories of our time together.

Or maybe you'd go and get all mushy and swoony over him and get your heart broken when he walked away.

Rolling out of bed, the icy silence of the world outside broken only by the scratching of an ice-covered branch against the window, I tried to ignore the thoughts.

Unsuccessfully.

It probably wasn't the best idea to get involved with Gannon.

I'd most likely end up with a bruised and broken heart, my loneliness even more prominent once he'd fucked me and high-tailed it back home.

But I couldn't help the draw I had to him. I'd felt it way back then and I felt it now. Like opposite poles of a magnet, there was something between us pulling, dragging, urging for more.

Or at least there was on my end.

I snorted softly. Leave it to me to get all worked up about whether or not hooking up with Gannon for a short time was a good idea when he likely wasn't even interested.

Not that I could blame him.

I wasn't anything like the guys he probably had hanging all over him in LA.

I started the kettle so we'd have hot water and shuffled sleepily to the bathroom to freshen up for the day. I'd likely be in pjs for most of it, but a quick wash and a brush of my teeth would make me feel more awake.

Deciding I'd treat my sexy guest to breakfast, I set to work.

Turning the oven to preheat, I popped two of Ginger's delicious cinnamon rolls onto a pan. She provided frozen rolls for cooking at home and they were *almost* as amazing as fresh-from-the-oven at the café.

After mixing a quick sugary, buttery icing for the rolls, I glanced in the fridge to assess my options.

I grabbed what usable veggies I had, a carton of eggs, cheese, ham, and butter.

Ham and veggie omelets for the main course.

Fishing two potatoes out of the bin, I set to work washing and peeling for a hash brown side.

Soon, the apartment was snuggly warm with heat from the oven and my heart bebopped along, just happy to be doing something nice for someone else.

Truly, helping others and taking care of those around me was what made me happy. Maybe it was my way of staying busy and not focusing on the bits and pieces missing— namely falling in love and being loved back—but I didn't think it was a bad way to move along the journey of life.

With the sun peeking over the horizon causing the world outside to sparkle under its thin layer of ice, I hummed softly, sautéing onions, mushrooms, peppers, spinach, and ham. As the hash browns sizzled and the cinnamon rolls baked, I whisked eggs and sipped my English Breakfast tea.

From the corner of my eye, I saw Gannon roll out of bed and stretch.

"Good morning," I said, realizing I was perhaps a bit too chipper when he winced and grunted. "Sorry." I grinned sheepishly. "Breakfast will be ready soon. Tea or hot chocolate?"

"Coffee?" Gannon's sleep-roughened voice went straight to my dick and I quickly turned toward the pantry hoping a perusal of my shelves would stave off the inopportune boner trying to make its presence known.

"Ummm," I stalled, pretending to search for Gannon's requested morning drink. "Yep! Found it." Turning, I held up the box of little coffee pods. "Coffee?" I asked with a cheeky grin.

While Gannon maybe didn't brighten the room with his smile, he at least gave a little huff of laughter. "Yes, please. Thought I'd have to trek to Ginger's," he said almost good-humoredly as he walked to the bathroom and closed the door behind him.

Five minutes later, the toilet flushed and Gannon joined me in the kitchen. He seemed a bit more awake and smelled of toothpaste, deodorant, and whatever product he'd run through his hair.

"Good thing I had coffee," I said, tossing him the pod and pointing toward the one-cup coffee maker in the corner. "Trekking to Ginger's would be ill-advised until the ice melts."

Gannon nearly gave himself whiplash jerking his head toward me. "What? What ice? What happened?"

I shrugged and pointed to the window. "Welcome to Saint Nicholas Crossing, the magical little Christmas town with wacky weather patterns."

He glanced out the window and the sound of a wounded animal escaped his gorgeous mouth. "What the hell? How the fuck am I supposed to get any work done now?"

I cocked my head. "No big deal, my Wi Fi here works even better than at the shop."

Gannon pinched the bridge of his nose. "That's not what I..." He sighed. "Just thought I'd take a bit of time away to work quietly, no distractions."

I pursed my lips, doing my best to ignore the sting of his words. "Promise not to be a distraction," I clipped out. "I've got work to keep me busy too. Not a child who expects to be entertained."

Gannon ran a hand through his hair. "That's not what I meant either. Sorry. I'm used to being on my own, used to things going my way. I'm not saying you're a distraction."

Hurt feelings slightly soothed, I nodded. "The clouds should clear here in a bit and the temps are supposed to get pretty nice today. The whole town shuts down pretty much anytime it ices—I personally think most people just enjoy a break from school and work, and a lot of us can continue our daily responsibilities pretty easily with our devices and internet. Everything should be back to normal by tomorrow."

Gannon cocked a brow. "Thought Christmas Town wouldn't be against a little winter weather."

I plated up breakfast, leaving the cinnamon rolls to cool on the stove, and gestured for him to sit. "Snow doesn't cause as much trouble as ice. Snow we can work with as long as it's not over a foot, but ice is a bitch."

Gannon gave one last look out the window before sitting down. "And you didn't know the ice was coming?"

Shaking my head, I took a bite of omelet. "Nah, like I said, we get weird weather here. Someone once compared it to being in a snow globe. Like, we don't get a lot of the same weather as the places around us—kinda like being protected —but we'll get snow, ice, and heavy rains that seem to end right at the edge of town."

Gannon chewed a bite of hash browns while he studied me. "So, you're saying Santa Claus Town gets wacky weather because someone picks it up and shakes it like a snow globe?"

I chuckled. "I know it sounds crazy, but sometimes it makes sense. When you've lived here long enough and seen the weather that the meteorologists never have much explanation for, sometimes it's just fun to chalk it up to the snow globe—or *bad weather* globe—theory and shrug it off." I watched as Gannon dug into his omelet like it was the tastiest thing he'd ever eaten—damn, wait until he got hold of Ginger's cooking—and my heart fluttered to know he appreciated the meal. "This one shouldn't steal too many days from us. We'll think positively and plan on heading up to your grandfather's place tomorrow."

"Any other bad weather supposed to hit?" Gannon asked.

Shaking my head, I took another bite. "That's not the way it works. We can watch their predictions, but we usually don't get what they call for. And we can get bad weather popping up in the blink of an eye—no warning from the weather channel."

"That's damn frustrating." Gannon frowned. "And weird." He huffed. "And kinda cool—if it wasn't such a disruption."

I grinned. "Agreed. Although, I've learned to just roll with it, so I'm more on Team Kinda Cool. I'm sure as someone who's used to sunny and warm all the time, it's more of a hard sell."

Gannon smirked. "The sunshine *is* nice, but I'm not gonna lie. I used to love coming here and experiencing the snow and thunderstorms. They were so far from what I knew, so exciting, and Grandpa always made a snowy day or thunderstorm seem like something special."

Emotion shone in Gannon's eyes as I nodded. "Weather days can either be a pain in the ass or something special. I choose to look at them as something special—kinda like a forced break and a chance to recharge. Not that we can't have school or work during a thunderstorm, but I take any and every opportunity to snuggle in and take a bit of time to relax. There's nothing quite like the soft, peacefulness of a fresh-fallen snow or the dark, rumbling intensity of a thunderstorm."

He looked at me for a moment, almost like I was a puzzle

he couldn't quite figure out, before nodding and returning to his food without a word.

We finished our breakfast in comfortable silence.

"Thanks for breakfast," Gannon said, standing and taking his plate to the sink, rinsing the food from it, and starting the disposal. "Sorry for—" He stopped abruptly when he turned and came chest-to-chest with me. His hands gripped my upper arms to keep me from stumbling backward. Clearing his throat, his eyes traveling from my lips to my eyes and back to my lips, he continued, "Sorry for making it seem like I thought you were a distraction. My peopling skills aren't the best."

Licking my lips, I nodded. "You're welcome. And don't worry about it. We all need a bit of space. You don't know me, I get it."

Gannon shook his head. "Nah, you've been nothing but kind and welcoming. I appreciate it." He looked at his hands on my arms and seemed to shake himself from a trance. "Sorry." He let go of me slowly. "So, um, what are your plans for the day?"

Smiling brightly, excited for the unexpected day at home, I said, "Finish lesson plans, record grades, watch the Christmas pageant tape and make notes, do a bit of notes and planning for The Heart—all while sipping eggnog or tea. Then I may indulge with a bubble bath. Definitely a movie."

"Damn, for a day off, that's a lot."

I shrugged. "It's a day *home*, not a day *off*. There's a difference."

"If it were truly *off*—and don't get me wrong, I wouldn't really know what to do if I weren't working on something—what would you do?"

"Easy. Bubble bath and then stay in bed all day reading and watching movies."

Gannon's eyes darkened and his nostrils flared.

Swallowing so his Adam's apple bobbed, he asked gruffly, "What kind of movies?"

My cheeks heated and I dipped my head. "This time of year, Christmas love stories, of course."

A chuckle burst from Gannon's lips. "Of course." He shook his head. "I should have known."

"What?" I teased. "I'm a gay boy in a tiny holiday town. I love love."

Gannon studied me intently. "Doesn't it bother you that the love story is always about a man and a woman?"

I shrugged. "Sometimes, but I just truly love watching the sappy happy endings and knowing the couple gets their forever. And a lot of the streaming channels are starting to make movies with more diversity. The one I watched last year had my little homo heart going all pitter-patter watching the guys fall in love and get their happily ever after. Although," I wrinkled my nose, "the supporting cast—especially the mother—was annoying as hell. Hoping for even better this year."

Gannon grunted. "Never seen a holiday movie with a gay couple—not that I watch any of them—"

"We can watch the one from last year while you're here."

Warning, warning my head screamed. *Don't get too excited about him being here. He's leaving. Thinking about asking him to fuck you is one thing. Showing him your sappy romance movies as a quiet winter wonderland surrounds your happy little abode is something very different.*

I ignored the thoughts.

"Do you like to read?" I asked, walking to my little bookshelf, not waiting for his answer. "I mostly read on my e-reader, but sometimes I love a book so much I order it in paperback." I searched for the title in question. "This one," I pulled out the wintery book and held it out to him, "is one of my all-time favorites. I stumbled upon it by accident because an author I read a lot of recommended it in their newsletter. *Holly Hills Christmas* is set in a small town a lot like Saint Nicholas Crossing so I was drawn in immediately. The guy on the front is hot and I quickly decided Kota and I would be friends—I actually spent about a week wishing he were real so I could meet him. Vince is the other main character," I paused to bite my knuckle and groan, "and hello silver fox daddy vibes. Ungh. I maybe packed him away for solo session fodder for the next six months at least."

I laughed at Gannon's wide eyes and waggled the book at him until he finally took it.

"They meet and things get steamy right away, but it's just a fling because Kota isn't staying. But it's a romance novel, so of course, feelings get involved. Maybe a bit of meddling from Kota's grandma. Sprinkle in a bit of Christmas magic—and funny scenes with a plant—and it's sexy, swoony, and so sweet. I've probably read it at least ten times."

"Am I going to find certain pages stuck together?" Gannon deadpanned.

Holding a hand to my throat, I gasped. "Did the grumpy visitor just break character to make a joke?"

Gannon huffed and smirked, flipping through the book.

"I'll have you know," I went on, smiling until my cheeks hurt all because I'd cracked this man just a tiny bit. "No bodily fluids were deposited in the book."

Gannon cocked a brow.

"No more talk of my bodily fluids unless you're going to tell me what you jack off to." I playfully pushed at his chest, making him *almost* laugh. "If you like to read and get lost in a love story, that's a good one. Maybe I liked it because it reminded me so much of this place. Or maybe because I wanted to be Kota's friend—and definitely wouldn't have minded a bit of alone time with Vince, but he's Kota's true love, so I won't break them up—" I bit my lip. "Sorry, I'm babbling. It's a good story. That author has another Christmas book and a bunch of other titles, I'm a fan."

"I don't really read…"

I went to grab the book back, but Gannon held it to his chest.

"But I might give this one a try. Definitely be the first romance I've ever read—and I didn't even know romance books had two guys falling in love."

My heart hurt for him. "First, there's an entire male/male romance subgenre—like, it's *huge*. At the risk of sounding like Aladdin, I could show you a whole new world." I shrugged, a bit self-conscious at how much I was rambling. "If you decide you'd like to read more books about guys falling in love. There are literally thousands upon thousands of titles to choose from—fantasy, sci-fi, contemporary, paranormal, historical…and the tropes are endless."

"Tropes?"

"Like enemies-to-lovers, best friend's brother, age gap, forced proximity, fated mates, arranged marriage, fake boyfriends, mafia, stuff like that. Readers have tropes they like and they read books with those tropes."

"Doesn't that make all the books the same?" Gannon's brow wrinkled as he studied my copy of *Holly Hills Christmas* in his hands.

"Not at all. The trope is the expected part—the happily ever after is required for romance, or at least a happy for now, don't let anyone tell you sad endings are romance— but the characters and stories are all very different depending on who is writing them. I bet you could give ten authors the same trope and they'd all write vastly different stories."

"So, what are the tropes in this one?" Gannon rolled his eyes. "And why am I even asking? Did you put something in my coffee?"

I laughed. "*You* made your coffee. Is the Christmas magic getting to you?"

He frowned. "There's no such thing as magic— Christmas or otherwise. I'm just off-kilter being in a new place."

"So, you don't want to know about the tropes in that book?" I asked, biting back my grin.

Gannon gritted his teeth. "Fine. Just so I know what I'm getting myself into. *If* I read it."

"Well, it's pretty steamy. I prefer romances with on-page sex rather than fade to black or closed door—probably because it's pretty much the only action I'm getting." I laughed. "It's got an age gap between the main characters. Kota is a lot younger than Vince."

Gannon's eyes bore into me and I wondered if he was thinking about the age gap between us—although ours was less than the one between Kota and Vince.

"It's set in a small town, so pretty much everyone knows everyone. There's also a bit of forced proximity, but it's not the whole book. It's holiday themed and, of course, a bit of holiday magic—"

"Which doesn't exist," Gannon interrupted.

"If you insist," I said. "Oh! One of my favorites—*there's only one bed.*"

"What?"

"When characters are forced to share a bed and things get all cuddly sweet before exploding into sexy heat."

Gannon gaped at me. "That's…that's not even a real thing. How many times have you been forced to share a bed with someone? Let alone forced to share a bed with someone you actually *want* to have sex with?"

I chuckled and patted his cheek. "It's fiction—an escape from reality—suspend your beliefs and just enjoy the swoony, chest-fluttering, love story."

Gannon huffed. "Maybe. I can't work *all* day, so I'll try a chapter if I get finished. And if I'm bored."

"No pressure. If you don't read it—or you do and you don't like it—I'll still count it as one of my favorites. And it won't stop me from loving romance novels—or sappy, cheesy holiday movies."

"Good. Shouldn't change yourself for others," Gannon mumbled, glancing at the book before walking toward his bed and tossing it on the pillow.

"That's often one of the things a main character learns in the books I read. Don't change yourself for love. Someone who truly loves you should love you just the way you are— scars, imperfections, weirdness, and all."

"Yeah," Gannon said. "Table up for grabs again?" he asked as he picked up his computer bag.

"Sure. If you don't mind sharing."

"All good. Going to put my earbuds in and get to work. I actually do have a phone call to make…"

No way was I letting a city-slicker from LA brave the icy steps in order to step out and make a call. "No worries. I'll go over to Mom and Dad's place here in a bit and check on them. You can make your call then." I checked the time. "I'll step out around ten. That's seven in LA, right? Will your friend be awake?"

Gannon snorted. "My administrative assistant. Yeah, Ellen will be up by five-thirty and working by six-thirty."

"Perfect."

Part of me wished I could stay to hear Gannon turn into full-on professional mode—what? Maybe the suit-and-tie, stern businessman thing did it for me from time to time— but I'd give him his privacy.

Plus, I did want to check in on Mom and Dad.

And see if they had the item I wanted to share with Gannon.

CHAPTER 5

Gannon

"WHY DO YOU SOUND WEIRD?" Ellen asked. She'd answered before the first ring ended and she knew something was up before I'd said ten words.

"What? I don't sound weird."

"You do. What's up?"

I sighed. There was never a reason to try to pull one over on Ellen.

She knew.

She *always* knew.

"This place is messing with my head," I said.

"You've been there one day," Ellen said, ever pragmatic. "What could be messing with you this quickly?"

I grunted and ran my hands through my hair. "Damned if I know. From the moment I drove into town, things felt…off."

"Off? How?"

Shaking my head as if she could see me, I huffed out a frustrated breath. "Wish I knew."

"You don't usually get rattled, Gannon. What's going on?

People don't like you? Out of place? They're mad at you selling?" Ellen rattled off possibilities.

"I've only met one person so far, he likes me fine, I guess. I *am* out of place, but it's not like anyone is unwelcoming— just the opposite in fact. It's almost like I've never felt so welcomed in a new place."

"*He* likes you just fine, huh?"

Ignoring her, I pushed on. "And they don't know I'm selling—well, not in a way where I've come straight out and said it, but I don't think Hayden has any idea. I mean, he *should*. What does he think I'm here for?"

"Hayden, huh?"

"Stop doing that."

"It's just cute. Hearing you so off-kilter and weird is strange enough, but knowing it's because of a guy is so sweet." Ellen was a force to be reckoned with in the professional world, but she was also a romantic at heart.

I groaned. "He's so fucking hot."

She seriously nearly squealed. "Tell me all about him."

"He's the farthest thing from the type of guy I usually go for."

"Thank god for that," she interrupted.

"What?"

"Gannon, you usually go for money-grubbing, materialistic pretty boys who couldn't hold a conversation if you handed it to them in a bucket. Tell me about this Hayden who has you so worked up."

"First, the weirdness is more than just Hayden. This place is weird."

I could almost see her nodding as Ellen replied, "It's the holiday magic, I guess."

"Oh god, not you too. There's no such thing as holiday magic."

"Sure there is," Ellen quipped. "I don't think everyone experiences it and maybe it's not *magic* magic, but there's always unexplainable things happening. Every moment of every day all around the universe. If you're feeling something special in that little Christmas town, I have no trouble chalking it up to magic—holiday or otherwise. Now, tell me about Hayden."

I winced at the dreamy sigh escaping my lips. "He's got this russet-colored hair. I can't figure out if he purposely styles it kinda out of control or doesn't even mess with it. His eyes are a dark grayish-blue, kinda like navy. His skin is pale with hints of freckles." I left out the part about his pretty, pink, kissable mouth and how I'd already jacked off thinking about his lips stretched around my cock. "And he wears these ridiculous suspenders and matching bowties— don't get me started on his socks and scarves. He's a teacher and volunteers at the store. He's cute and funny and helpful and so damn nice." I glanced out the window. "If he comes back, I'll have to stop talking about him."

"Comes back? Where are you?"

"I slept at his place."

"What?! Gannon, don't corrupt the poor kid."

"In his spare bed. The car I rented can't make it up the hill on ice, Hayden couldn't take me up due to a fallen tree, and the little motel is full. He offered me a bed. We were supposed to head up the hill to my grandfather's place today, but it iced last night—with no warning, by the way, I guess this place gets wacky weather patterns or something. Anyway, he lives in the garage apartment at his parents' place and he went down to check on them so I could make my call in private."

"Awwww, he sounds delightful."

"He's gorgeous, but it's more than that and I don't like it."

Ellen clucked. "You don't like that you've met a gorgeous,

caring man who puts up with your shit and doesn't mind having you around? Yes, I can see how that would be just terrible."

I huffed and flopped down on the bed. "I don't like the instant draw I felt to him and this place. I *really* don't like the unexplainable shit around here—don't like feeling like I'm under some kinda spell. Don't like that the weather can't be predicted." I paused and huffed out a sigh. "And back to Hayden. Why do I feel so connected to him? I'm not going as far as to say *love* at first sight, but I definitely feel something between us—more than just physical attraction. I don't like it."

"You don't like that you've met someone so different from your usual guys and now you're getting ready to ruin the possibility of anything between the two of you by selling the hub of their sweet little Christmas town?" Ellen offered softly.

I grunted. "Yeah, *that*." Ellen was truly the only person I'd ever let in enough—okay, she'd kinda just stuck her foot in the door and pushed her way in—to trust her with my true feelings.

"Do you have to sell the store?"

"It's what I do. It's what I came here for."

"But do you *have* to?"

"What else would I do with it?"

"I'm just offering options."

Another grunt escaped my lips. "I'm only here for a week, I don't think options are necessary. I'm here to get things organized and sell. I'll be gone before they know it."

"Maybe you should stay a bit longer?" Ellen said.

"What? Why would I stay here *longer*? I'm already fucked up being here."

"Despite the weirdness—which I think a lot of seems to be just *feeling* something, an act we both know you do your best to steer clear of—I think you need a break from LA." She went on, ignoring my attempted interruption. "Gannon, you can work from anywhere. You have no attachments here. You don't even *like* most people here. I haven't heard you like this in…well, in forever. Stick around. Get to know the town your grandpa devoted his life to. Get to know the people he called friends."

"No one around here is going to want me in town when they realize I'm selling the store."

"So, don't make any snap decisions. Watch and learn. If the store is doing good things, making a profit, why not let it continue?"

"I didn't come here to become a general store shop owner."

"No, you went there to assuage your guilt and make some money—which you're not in need of, but maybe the folks around there *are*," Ellen snapped. Leave it to her to tell me exactly how it was. "Give yourself a breather. Have a bit of fun with Hayden. You don't have a deadline outside of the self-imposed one. I'll check on your apartment from time-to-time, we'll continue with our phone or video check-ins, you can work from there—assuming you have internet—"

I snorted. "Yeah, Holiday Town has better internet than LA."

"Perfect. Let's just let things go for a bit. See how you feel after a few days. Hell, maybe you even decide to keep Joseph's place and use it as a little getaway when you need a break."

"Yeah, that's not happening," I said, rolling my eyes.

Ellen made an annoyed sound, but she let it go.

We switched over to business talk—as usual, I wasn't surprised Ellen had everything handled perfectly on her end —and ended the call about ten minutes later.

I'd been working about fifteen minutes when Hayden

breezed through the door, a gust of cold air behind him. "Good news, the ice is already starting to melt thanks to the sunshine. We should be good to go for the trek up the hill tomorrow."

"And bad news?"

"What?"

"Good news, bad news?"

Hayden laughed. "Nope, just good news."

I grunted, not used to the constant cheerfulness—but not hating it, especially in conjunction with his cute smile.

We worked in comfortable silence for about two hours, but I finally had to throw in the towel. I was tapped out on spreadsheets and numbers, offers and counter-offers.

Slamming my computer shut, wincing when Hayden jumped at the noise, I stood and stretched. "Sorry, I just can't do anymore work."

"Oh, thank god," Hayden said with a chuckle. "I've finished two weeks of lesson plans, reviewed the children's pageant, and made notes for the store. I'm ready to veg out with a movie, but I didn't want to interrupt you."

"I'm in your space, don't change your routine because of me."

Hayden grinned. "I like having someone here—" He blushed. "Makes me feel not so alone."

Well, if that didn't make my stomach do flip-flops. I didn't like this gorgeous man feeling alone—*being* alone—and my chest squeezed with the idea *I* could make sure he wasn't alone.

Even if just for a little bit.

But what then? What happened when I went back to LA? Hayden was left alone again?

And you're right back to being aloof, detached, and alone—just the way you like it, right?

We settled in with one of Hayden's cheesy holiday

romance movies—one with a same-sex couple—and, even though I had to roll my eyes a lot, it was actually kinda cute.

"Makes me wonder how much easier things would have been if movies like this existed when I was a kid," I mused as the credits rolled.

Hayden poured himself another glass of eggnog. "Right. I mean, I feel like each generation gets a little easier—and I didn't have it *bad* coming out here—but seeing yourself represented in the mainstream has to be so good for so many people."

"I swear, that's like the never-ending pitcher of eggnog," I teased. "How many of those have you had?"

"Eggnog magic," he said with a giggle. If I didn't know better, I would have thought he'd been adding brandy to each serving. He held up his glass. "It's so good. Don't you want to taste it?"

"No," I said, wrinkling my nose and shaking my head. "I'm good." I *wanted* to taste *him*, but I kept that little tidbit to myself.

"More for me," Hayden crowed. "I'm going to shower, then I have something I want to show you from my parents' place."

I nodded, trying my best to *not* think about a naked, wet Hayden. Did the freckles continue below his clothes? Was that sexy little trail of hair beneath his waistband the same pretty russet color?

Hayden headed toward the bathroom and I idly picked up *Holly Hills Christmas*. I hadn't read a fiction title in years, and definitely never a romance novel, but I found myself turning to the first page as Hayden turned on the shower.

Twenty minutes later, Hayden walked out of the bathroom and I held up the book. "Mary Joy is scheming, isn't she?"

Hayden blinked and grinned. "Maybe."

"I like Kota already. I guess I'd be this Vince character since I'm older and kinda grinch-y."

"How far did you read?" Hayden asked.

"Just the first two chapters."

"It keeps getting better—and, um, kinda *hot*, just a warning."

"Like porn-on-a-page? Not that there's anything wrong with porn," I said hastily.

"Agreed, nothing wrong with porn, I enjoy it," Hayden said, grinning through his blush. "But no, *Holly Hills* is a holiday romance with on-page sex throughout a story—real connections between the main characters, a happily ever after. Porn-on-a-page would be more like erotica—mostly just sex, probably no true love, no happily ever after, maybe not even a *story* as far as plot and character arc."

I smiled. "Do you get this into explaining things to your students?"

His blush deepened. "Maybe?"

"It's nice. Makes me want to read more. Probably does the same for your students, they're lucky to have you."

Just when I thought he'd wave away the compliment, Hayden paused. "Thank you. That's really nice. Everyone around here says I'm a good teacher, and I know the kids like me, but it's nice to hear it from someone who hasn't known me all my life."

I nodded. "I get that."

Hayden gestured toward the couch. "Mom and Dad had this picture book Saint Nicholas Crossing put together about ten years ago. I thought you might want to look at it."

"Wow, that's huge," I said, taking the spiral-bound book from Hayden.

Hayden choked back a giggle and I cocked a brow.

"Sorry, my head's in the gutter."

I thought back to what I'd said and rolled my eyes with a

grunt of laughter as I attempted to will my dick *not* to get hard. "Is the jolly little helper a size queen?" I teased, the rusty skill creaking a bit as I put it to use after so many years.

Hayden's eyes went wide and his cheeks pinked. "Not really." He shrugged. "Around here, a guy can't be too picky. Big, small, and in-between, I'm usually just glad for some action."

A white-hot streak of jealousy shot through me at the idea of Hayden with other guys. I wanted to pull him close, kiss him senseless, and claim him as *mine*.

Which was so damn unheard of—I didn't *do* committed relationships, didn't *do* possessiveness. But I wanted Hayden all to myself.

Instead, I cleared my throat. "So, no long-term boyfriends?"

Hayden snorted. "Not in the least. Even in the city, I couldn't really find anyone I wanted to stick around. Maybe I was trying too hard."

"What do you look for in a partner?" Maybe if I heard how *not-his-type* I was, my stupid head and heart—and dick— would calm themselves and get rid of the ridiculous notion of Hayden and I together.

Hayden cocked his head. "Umm," his forehead wrinkled, "dang, it's been so long since I thought about what I want outside of just a physical release." He bit his lip. "That makes me sound like a slut, I promise I'm not."

"Nothing wrong with finding someone to help you scratch an itch," I said, completely meaning it while still wishing with every fiber of my being that I'd never have to think of Hayden with other guys.

"If I'm describing my fantasy guy, he's someone who supports me—makes me a priority—and takes care of me. Like, he makes me take time for myself." He shrugged. "I know I sometimes get too wrapped up in staying busy and helping others. I want someone to love me enough to make me put myself first sometimes." He dropped his head in his hands. "That sounds pathetic."

I gripped his wrist and pulled his hand away from his face. "Not pathetic."

Hayden snorted. "You're not sitting there admitting you need a man to help you put yourself first."

"Nah, I'm pretty damn good at thinking only of myself," I said wryly. "But I wouldn't turn down a guy who needs me, someone who wants me around for *me* and not what I can do for them because of my money or social circles."

What the fuck was wrong with me? I didn't tell people shit like that.

"Well, we're quite the pair, huh?" Hayden said.

"That we are. Let's look at these pictures before I give in to whatever drugs this place is hazing me with and spill all of my deepest, darkest secrets."

Hayden smiled. "No drugs, but that holiday magic can really do a number on ya."

"Maybe if I believed in it."

He shook his head, still grinning. "Nope. Doesn't work that way. In fact, I sometimes think it hits the non-believers even harder." Hayden leaned close, cupping my face, and whispered, "Just give in to it. Let it overtake you," he cooed, his eyes sparkling. "It'll feel so good."

Fuck. I knew he was joking around and talking about magic, but his words, the soft croon of his voice, had my dick stirring. I wanted to lean in and capture those pretty pink lips.

Instead, I forced a laugh and turned my head to open the book on my lap. "Never. I won't be taken down by holiday magic."

"If you say so," Hayden teased. "Honestly, though, sometimes it's just easier to believe."

We dove into the photobook, which was a compilation of photos and captions as far back as when my grandfather was a teenager.

"Your grandpa was kinda hot," Hayden said, pointing to a photo of Joseph at a town festival dance.

"Objectively speaking, yes. As his grandson, don't ever use the word hot and grandpa in the same sentence again," I said with a grimace.

Hayden giggled and poured more eggnog.

I picked up the insulated pitcher and glanced inside. "I swear, it's never ending. Do you have a secret stash you keep adding to it?"

He shook his head, eyes alight as he sipped from his cup. "Maaagic," he whispered before snorting at my eye roll.

Joseph was in many photos from his teen years until the printing of the book. Always pitching in to help, always smiling, always surrounded by friends. My heart clenched to know I'd missed out on so much of that. A sour swirl filled my gut knowing how different I was from my grandfather.

He'd told me he never understood how his son could be so cold and so much the exact opposite of himself. Was I the same type of confusing disappointment as my father had been?

When I was a boy, Joseph had done his best to instill that helpful, giving spirit in me. But I'd gone and turned out more like my father—cold, detached, more interested in money and success than in the heart of humanity.

Those are things that can change, but you have to be willing.

"What are you thinking?" Hayden asked as I studied a more recent photo of Joseph helping children shop for clothes and toys.

"Just that I hate to think I let him down," I said, trying to fight off the sting of sadness and vulnerability the words delivered.

"How's that?"

"I'm nothing like him. I don't help, I don't care for others, I don't have friends who are better for knowing me." I shook my head. "I'm more and more like my father with each passing year and that's something that Joseph would be so damn sad to see."

Hayden pushed the book to the side and turned to face me. "No, I don't see it that way. I get that we barely know each other, but Joseph talked about you a lot—and even in the short time I've known you, I have this gut feeling. You're not your father. True, I only have stories to go by, but I know he wasn't anything like Joseph—one of life's great mysteries how a kid from two good people could turn out so cold and rotten. And maybe you're not just like Joseph, but that's okay because you can work on those things. You can be Gannon Snow—Joseph's grandson who continues his grandfather's good work in his own unique ways." He took my hand, heat sparking between us as my heart and head battled over his words. "You don't have to do good deeds the exact same as Joseph. Do them your way."

I shook my head. "I don't think my heart knows how to do good anymore. I'm not a *bad* guy, I just haven't ever found myself with the same giving spirit Joseph had." Frowning, I rubbed at my chest. "He was so generous, so *good*. My dad was an ass. And now, here I am following in his footsteps."

Hayden squeezed my hand. "So, change the path. Veer away from your dad's footsteps—you don't have to fit your feet into Joseph's prints, you can make your own way."

"How?"

He cocked his head. "I don't think there's one right answer for that. It'll come to you if you're open to it. Don't go searching for ways to do good, just let your heart take in what's around you—the universe will show you where you're needed." He shrugged. "At least, that's the way it feels to me."

"I could donate money…"

Hayden nodded. "You could, and it would be much appreciated. But I think Gannon Snow has more to offer than just money. You just need to let it happen."

"Let what happen?"

"The holiday magic, of course," Hayden teased.

I groaned.

"No, for real," he went on. "Joseph regretted his son's decisions and how things ended between them, but he never once had anything but hopeful, positive things to say about you. Used to talk about how you'd gone a bit astray, but he had faith you'd end up right back where you belonged, doing exactly what the universe needed you to do." Hayden absently ran his thumb over my knuckles. "I know I'm younger, but from the time I was able to recognize the pride and joy in his words, I knew Joseph Snow loved you and had high hopes for all the good you'd do in life."

"And now I'm nearly forty and what have I done? Made money, built a business, purchased a bunch of shit that doesn't matter, and done absolutely nothing of real importance when it comes to people in need." I fought the inexplicable urge to cuddle close to Hayden and let his warmth push away the guilt and self-loathing. "I hate that he's gone and I didn't get to say goodbye—didn't spend enough time with him. Always too busy being focused on my own successes."

"It was easier to focus on success—you can be cold and detached in that area. It's harder to open yourself up, be vulnerable, let yourself be led to where you're most needed, where you'll be able to do the most good."

I scoffed. "And you think it's my lot in life to hunker down in Saint Nicholas Crossing and run the general store?"

My head wanted to argue—I couldn't even *consider* staying here—but my heart kept whispering, *"When was the last time you felt this good? Even though it's confusing, you've never been this relaxed and free from worries."*

Hayden shrugged. "That's not for me to say. I know we'd be happy to have Joseph's grandson here in town to continue with his grandfather's helpful, giving spirit, but that has to be a decision *you* make—has to be something your heart is called to do. There's more to be done than just working at the store—more even than staying in this tiny town if it's not what you feel in your heart is best for you."

"So, you think I should leave?"

Hayden huffed. "Not saying that, either. Selfishly," he paused, swallowing and meeting my eyes, "I'd really like you to stay."

God, I wanted that. Wanted to forget about everything else, stay hidden away at St. Nicholas Crossing, lose myself in this beautiful man.

Everything in me begged to lean in and kiss Hayden. To devour his lips, explore his mouth, give in to the longing and desire.

But where would that leave me?

I'd still need to sell the store.

Still need to return to my business in LA.

And everything would be complicated by a sexual entanglement I was one hundred percent sure neither Hayden nor I needed.

Tearing my eyes from his, I looked back at the photobook. "Who are they?" I asked, pointing to a picture of Joseph with two women. Grandpa looked to be about fifty-ish—so, well after my father had left town without looking back—and the women looked to be around thirty. The trio glowed with happiness, broad, mischievous smiles on their faces.

"Ginger and Candy. Lifelong residents—although, I think

both left at one time or another to follow partners, but both ended up back here and swear they learned their lesson and will never leave again," Hayden explained. "They are as much the backbone of this town as Joseph was. Ginger runs the Ginger Snap Café and Candy started Candy Cane Counter. They both also cook and serve lunches in the cafeteria at school. They're getting up there in years, but you'd never know it from their spunky personalities."

I read the caption of the photo. "Never stop taking time for fun and exploration. Oh, the stories these smiles could tell."

Cocking a brow, I glanced at Hayden. "Did the three of them have something going on?"

He smirked. "I think so. I know Ginger and Candy are best friends, but they're also a bit more than that. Committed to each other, but open to others joining in is my understanding. I think they had something going with Joseph from around the time of this picture until he passed—the three of them were tight, always working together to help people in town, but also taking time to tuck themselves away up on the hill and recharge." Hayden bit his lip. "Can you imagine the stories? I'm sure Ginger and Candy would be happy to talk to you."

Shuddering, I pulled a face. "Yuck, I have no desire to hear about my grandpa's threesome."

Hayden giggled and took another drink of his never-ending eggnog. "I didn't mean talk to you about sex stories. Just tell you about Joseph, fill you in on the times you missed out on."

"Basically an entire lifetime," I muttered.

"Maybe, but that doesn't mean it's not worth learning about." He bumped my shoulder. "I'm sure it's weirding you out—"

I bumped back and cocked a brow. "*Weirding* me out?"

He shrugged. "Creeping you out, setting you on edge, whatever. I know we barely know each other, but I meant it when I said we'd be happy to have you stay. *I'd* be happy to have you stay. Maybe you can't hang around forever, but it feels like...I don't know...probably sounds crazy, but it feels like I've known you my whole life and I kinda want more time—even though I know you don't like it here and eventually *have* to leave."

"It's not so much that I don't like it here—I have really great memories of this place." Why in the hell was I explaining myself to someone I barely knew?

Because you trust him and you feel the same weird connection he does. Maybe there's no real reason or explanation, but that doesn't mean it's not there.

I went on. "It's just sad that Joseph is gone and I'm having to admit how much I screwed up in leaving and not coming back before he died. This place brings back happy times, but it also brings memories of the bad shit I came here to escape when I was younger. And," I gave him a wink, "holiday magic or not, this town has me acting out of character and feeling shit I don't like to feel."

"Like what?" Hayden asked.

Anyone else would have gotten a huff and a view of my back as I walked away—well, anyone but Ellen.

And evidently Hayden had joined that exclusive club because I sighed and said, "Connections."

My eyes met his and there was no mistaking the desire; Hayden was just as interested in me as I was in him.

And that was dangerous.

Not because of the potential heat combusting between us, but because I felt more for this guy than...well, than anyone before him, if I were being honest.

It wasn't as if I'd never had nameless, meaningless hookups with strangers I'd met in hotel bars late at night.

But Hayden wasn't nameless.

He wasn't my type.

I was in town for a week—that would be more than a quick hookup.

And I got the feeling Hayden wasn't the type of guy I could fuck out of my system—especially if we ended up in bed most of the week. He was addictive, I already knew that just from the short time knowing him.

Continuing, because it seemed to be what Hayden expected, I said, "I don't like emotions—mostly because the bad has to come with the good. So, I keep them both out by being detached and aloof. LA is great because I can do that. I'm a tiny, meaningless blip on the radar out there. Here, I feel seen." I shook my head, trying to make sense of my own words. "And it's shaking me up—but more than that, I feel at home and that's throwing me off the most."

"You *are* home, if you want to be," Hayden said. "This town may be silly to some, just a throw-away to others, but we take care of our own and we welcome those in need with open arms."

Bristling, I clipped out, "I'm not in need."

Hayden placed a hand on my arm. "Maybe not financially, but there are other types of need. You're part of us because you're Joseph's grandson. Maybe you're here because you need closure on what you had with him. Or maybe coming here will eventually help you put an end to the rocky mess you had with your parents. Hell, maybe you're just here because your heart needs to feel like it belongs."

As if sensing he'd ventured way too far, too quickly into things deeper than I wanted to do delve, Hayden nudged my knee and smirked over his glass of eggnog. "Or maybe you just came here so a certain jolly little helper with an eggnog problem can show you a good time."

"Eggnog addiction and an issue with bowties and

suspenders," I teased, trying my best not to wonder if Hayden's mention of *a good time* had any sexual connotations or if it was just my dick having high hopes.

Hayden feigned offense with a hand to his throat. "I'll have you know, my crazy, bold socks, colorful scarves, and bowties with matching suspenders are a huge hit around town, thank you very much."

Smiling, I took the change in subject, relieved to move away from anything having to do with emotions and trying to figure out if coming onto Hayden was worth the upheaval I had no doubt would come along with it.

"How many of each do you think you have?" I asked.

Hayden grinned broadly as if happy to discuss his fashion accessories. "Scarves, probably about thirty. It's about fifty-fifty on store-bought and handmade. Ginger and Candy make most of them or I buy on small business websites. Socks, probably over one hundred. I can't resist. I'll see them and have this impulse to buy—the crazier or more outlandish, the better. Most of the time, I don't even know what I'm going to wear them with, I just need to have them.

"The bowties came first, so I have more of them. But once I realized there were often suspenders to match the ties, all bets were off and I had to have every single pair known to man. I'm probably almost there—might have about a hundred bowties, eighty pairs of suspenders?"

My eyes went wide. "I didn't know there was such a market for matching bowties and suspenders."

Hayden laughed. "I probably keep it in business single-handedly, but Ginger and Candy make a lot of them for me. I'll tell them the pattern or colors I want and they can whip 'em up in a couple days once they get the fabric. I mostly do Christmas and winter patterns, but I have other holidays. If I'm wearing my loud socks, I'll make sure to wear calmer ties and suspenders. If I do patterned up top, I'll keep the socks more subdued."

"And the scarves?"

"Those are fair game since they're usually on the outside. I'll try to wear a different scarf throughout all of winter, switching them on a rotating schedule. Sometimes, I wear one as a fashion statement. Mostly though, it's out of necessity and I don't care what they look like as long as they're warm."

Hayden's phone buzzed and he read the text. "Looks like we'll be good to go up the hill tomorrow. We can leave early so we'll have the whole day to work."

My head jerked to his. "Oh, I don't expect you to stay and work." Not that I would mind having Hayden by my side as I sifted, sorted, organized, but I wasn't in town for him to give up his time.

"No worries. I don't teach tomorrow and Mom and Dad can cover the store." He bit his lip. "Unless you just don't want me there? I figured it could be kinda overwhelming, maybe a friend being there would help."

I started to protest.

Started to tell him I was perfectly capable of tackling the job on my own.

But the unfamiliar swirl of swoony warmth I felt toward this man wrapped around my words and before I knew it I was saying, "Sure, that sounds great. I'd appreciate it."

What in the ever-loving hell was wrong with me?

Gannon Snow didn't need help.

He didn't *do* overwhelmed or emotional or appreciation.

Yeah, that probably made me a dick—okay, yes, it made me a dick—but it was the easiest way to get from Point A to Point B with zero issues—no entanglements, no regrets—and I didn't like the way this town and this man were messing with my head.

And my heart.

No regrets? Really?

Okay, fine. I had regrets.

But that was only because I'd let myself get emotionally involved with my grandpa before realizing all of those feelings and good times and memories were just little timebombs waiting to explode and bring pain.

"Great, we'll throw on our warmest winter gear and head out first thing." Hayden's feet—covered in wildly-patterned socks, of course—tapped happily on the coffee table. "Should be fun—an adventure."

Shutting down the desire and excitement churning in my chest, I cleared my throat. "If by fun adventure you mean sifting through my dead grandfather's personal effects, sure." I was being a dick, but it was easier than thinking about spending another day with Hayden without yanking him into my arms and kissing him senseless.

His face fell. "Right. Damn, that was insensitive of me. I'm sorry."

I stood and stretched, noticing how the sun was already setting. Damn, how many hours had we whittled away together on the couch? Waving away Hayden's apology, hoping to ease the awkwardness I'd brought to the room, I said, "I don't exactly have winter gear. I have jeans and a sweater, will those do?"

Hayden's eyes went wide. "Not if you want to keep your fingers and toes safe from frostbite. I'd hate to see that perfect ass freeze to death up on the hill." He waggled his brow and I decided I liked the flirty side of Hayden Green. "Tomorrow, we'll go to the store and get you outfitted with winter gear. You'll get to see how much good The Heart does for folks."

He rinsed his glass and placed it in the dishwasher.

"I'm going to take the book back to my parents. I'll

probably stay for a bit and visit so you're on your own. There's food in the pantry—or you're welcome to come with me and eat dinner over there."

That thought had me almost breaking out in hives. Meeting the parents? People who knew Joseph their whole lives? The Greens would have known about me ever since Joseph first had me come visit.

No, I didn't want to meet them and have dinner with them.

Eventually, you'll have to. Whether for business reasons or because you allow yourself to admit you've got a thing for their son.

I cleared my throat, pushing away my ridiculous thoughts —I did *not* have a thing for their son, no matter how cute and flirty he was. No matter how much my dick thought it needed to get involved. And no matter how fluttery-weird he made my heart feel. "I'm good, thanks. Probably going to read and take a shower. I'll be ready in the morning."

Hayden studied me for a moment before nodding. "Yeah, sounds good. See you in the morning."

As he headed toward the door, I called out, "Thanks for the pictures. Tell your parents thanks as well. It was good looking through them."

Had it been good? Seeing Joseph had stirred things in me —things I'd effectively shut down over the past several years. Feelings I didn't want to experience. But the pictures, the glimpse into my grandpa's life and the important part he played in this town had brought me a connection to him—to this place—I hadn't known I longed for.

And what are you going to do with that connection?

Scoffing at my meddling mind, I watched Hayden head out the door.

Nothing. I was going to do nothing with that connection.

It wasn't like I could leave LA, leave my business, and waltz into town like I thought I could replace Joseph.

Even if I wanted to do any of those things, I couldn't.

You have nothing keeping you in LA.

Hello, my *job?*

You can work from anywhere. Hell, the company basically runs on its own already. You've got good people and real estate isn't going away any time soon. Start something else here—a lot of untapped potential in the surrounding towns and cities.

Didn't matter that I could work anywhere. What the hell would I do in St. Nicholas Crossing? Pretend to be as great as Joseph while people laughed behind my back at how pathetic I was?

No one would expect you to be Joseph. You could carry on his generosity and helpful, giving spirit in your own way.

Ignoring my mixed-up head, I absentmindedly ate a bowl of cereal before collapsing on my bed and opening the book Hayden had given me.

Thirty minutes later, I hauled myself to the bathroom where I proceeded to angrily jerk off to an image of Hayden thanks to the steamy scene I'd read in the book.

I hated being in this place.

Hated the long-buried emotions fighting their way to the surface.

Hated the swirl of thoughts messing with my head.

Hated the hot desire coursing through me for a guy I barely knew.

Even hated the damn hot love story I'd found myself enamored with.

But mostly, I hated that I maybe didn't hate any of it as much as I wanted to pretend I did.

Damn the crazy little Christmas town magic.

Not that I believed in that shit.

CHAPTER 6

Hayden

I WAS in way over my head.

Gannon Snow was like no one I'd ever met.

He wasn't more attractive than other guys I'd known. He wasn't the most successful person I'd ever met—and truly, what constituted success? He was grumpy and aloof—kinda prickly—but I couldn't help the feelings he stirred deep inside.

Maybe it was because I sensed something so much more in him. Maybe it was because I'd longed for a real connection most of my adult life and there was *something* between Gannon and me.

I didn't know if it was the holiday magic or a natural connection or a little bit of both, but I had it bad for Gannon and I wasn't quite sure what to do about it.

The little bit of flirting had been easy and he hadn't balked, but I was certain no man like Gannon would want anything to do with a small-town guy like me. I had nothing to offer him.

You have you to offer him and that's more than enough.

Scoffing as I rolled from bed long before sunrise, I quietly made my way to the shower so I could be in and out before Gannon needed the bathroom.

I loved St. Nicholas Crossing. Loved the good we did for people. Loved my little happy life—even though that whole love-of-a-lifetime was missing. But me loving what I had wasn't going to be enough for a guy like Gannon.

How do you know? Maybe you leave that up to him to decide.

As the hot water rained down on me, I thought of Gannon. True, I didn't know him well, but the detached persona seemed to be a front—a way of protecting himself. I got the feeling he'd learned to block out *all* emotions so as to avoid the painful ones, but he couldn't hide them completely.

The pictures of Joseph had affected him.

Gannon had a lot of guilt over staying away.

Pain and regret over losing his grandpa.

Anger at his parents if the bits and pieces of what Joseph said about his estranged son were anywhere close to accurate. The older man had always been concerned about what Gannon was exposed to in his parents' toxic marriage.

And I had this feeling Gannon was also fighting a lot of fear.

Fear over not knowing how to handle the way he felt in St. Nicholas Crossing.

Fear over not knowing what his future held.

I'd bet money uncertainty was running rampant and I doubted Gannon knew how to deal with feeling uncertain.

He was the type of guy who made a plan, executed the plan, kept his heart out of it, and moved on.

St. Nicholas Crossing had gotten to him. Our little town had dug its claws into his self-made cold heart and started the melting process. Gannon would fight it. He'd hate it. But this place usually got what it wanted, and if it wanted Joseph's grandson, there was very little he could do about it in the long run.

Selfishly, I wanted him to give in to what our little Christmas town wanted.

I wanted him to stay.

Wanted him to let this place seep into his bones, wrap its loving fingers around his heart, and wash over him like a warm, comforting blanket.

And I wanted him to feel for me what I felt for him.

It didn't make sense to be gone for him so quickly.

And it wasn't just a physical attraction—although, that was strong as hell and had me wanting to jump his bones the moment he indicated he'd be down with it.

But there was this heart connection, too.

Something I'd never had with any guy I'd dated.

Never had with any of the random hookups.

A feeling that our hearts wanted to be together.

That they'd found their homes here with each other if only we'd be open to it.

Living in a magic little town or not, the feelings were throwing me for a loop.

I wanted to act on them. Wanted them to be real. Wanted to know Gannon felt them too.

But I also knew he had no plans to stay. I needed to protect my heart. Keep my emotions in check and not allow myself to dream about something that probably would never be.

When I walked out of the bathroom, a sleepy Gannon sat up in bed, the book I'd loaned him open as he read. "Why do I like this book so much?"

I winked with a smile. "Because you're a closet romantic who loves love and thrives on happily ever afters—plus you're horny and the sex is steaming hot."

Gannon's cheeks flushed and I knew he'd definitely been enjoying the sex scenes. "It feels dumb because I know they aren't real, but I can't help rooting for them."

"That's the great thing about romance, you know they'll get a happy ending. But reading how they get there is the fun part."

He returned to the book as I made tea and started a cup of coffee for Gannon.

I heard him close the bathroom door and the shower turn on a few minutes later. I couldn't help but wonder if he stroked himself off like I did while standing under the warm spray. What were the chances he thought of me while jerking off like I thought of him? Maybe he wasn't the type to jack off in a shower not his own. Or maybe he controlled himself better than me.

Maybe thinking of him jerking off isn't the wisest right now.

Shaking my head, I forced the thoughts away before he walked into the kitchen and found me with an erection tenting my flannel pants.

"Can we make it up the hill?" Gannon asked a bit later as he came into the kitchen and immediately grabbed the cup of coffee.

Fighting off the pang of how badly I wanted him in my kitchen every morning—how easily I could imagine it—I nodded. "Yep, Dad's already heard from someone who heard from someone that the road is clear. A warm breeze blew in last night and finished the melting process the afternoon sun had started—ice is clear." I glanced at his designer jeans and sweater. "We'll head to the store and get you a warm coat and accessories so you won't be cold at Joseph's. I think the heat has been turned off, but the electric is probably still on. We'll take some heaters with us. The house hasn't been empty for long, so I'm sure there are blankets and whatnot. We'll take some groceries so you'll have food while you're there."

"Not planning on taking too long. Just have to get everything together, figure out what's going where, and take care of business." Gannon glanced at me as if worried he'd let something slip. "Need to head out by the end of the week."

My heart sank, but I scolded myself for allowing the disappointment.

I'd known Gannon didn't plan on staying.

It was pointless to be upset by it.

Maybe the deadline means you can have a fun little hookup with no strings before he leaves.

"We'll take Dad's truck," I said.

"I don't want to put him out of a vehicle," Gannon answered with a frown.

"Nah, he's got another one he and Mom share. They usually drive to the store together, anyway. Plus, it's warmer today so they might walk."

"It's warmer, but you're dressing me in winter gear?"

I shrugged. "You're a California boy," I teased. "Not used to anything under seventy, right?"

Gannon huffed. "Sometimes the overnight and early morning temps can get down in the forties, it's not like I've never been around cold temperatures."

I grinned. "Well, it's around fifty right now—luckily, since we needed the ice to melt—but it could easily be below freezing in the next day or so. Never know when snow will dump down. And if the wind picks up, the temps will feel even colder. If you don't *want* warm winter gear, that's fine."

Gannon narrowed his eyes. "I'll take the winter gear."

"Perfect, let's go."

We piled into Dad's truck, Gannon with his overnight bag which made me sad to think he wouldn't be sleeping at my place again.

I navigated the truck through the quiet streets—the town just waking up for the day—and parked behind St. Nick's Heart.

"What time does the shop open?" Gannon asked.

"Within the hour. Sometimes we'll get folks dropping in early if we open the doors. The café brings people in early and they usually come over to shop when they finish eating."

I'd skipped my bowtie and suspenders for the day since I was in jeans and a sweatshirt, but my signature colorful scarf and loud socks under my winter boots made me feel cute as I unlocked the backdoor and led Gannon inside. I didn't wear the socks and scarves to impress others, but having someone I wanted to look good for was rare enough, I figured I'd take advantage and enjoy.

"Okay, winter boots instead of designer boots are a must. Winter coat, scarf, hat, and gloves. If I can find a pair of snow pants, those would be good if you plan to work outside."

Gannon shook his head. "Probably not this time. May have to do outside work on a different visit. Don't want to take snow pants from someone who really needs them."

"Awww, the grumpy visitor's heart is thawing as his generous spirit comes through," I teased, bumping my hip against his.

Gannon snorted. "Outfit me, oh happy helper."

About ten minutes later, I led Gannon to our little dressing room and handed him a coat and boots. "Try these on. The scarf, hat, and gloves aren't an issue, but we need to make sure these fit."

I puttered around a bit while Gannon pulled on the boots and coat—both of which he'd demanded be gently-used rather than any of our brand-new options so he wasn't taking from anyone who really needed them...and, of course, my heart melted even more for the man.

"Those going to work? Need a different size?" I called from the other side of the curtain.

Gannon opened the curtain and stood there looking like a winter-wet-dream with his dark hair sprinkled in silver, his grey-blue eyes steady on me as I took him in, and his strong jean-clad legs looking sexy as hell with the snow boots. "I think they both work. Coat is really warm, and the boots are only slightly big—maybe need some thicker socks."

Without thinking, I stepped close and pulled the collar of the coat up around his ears. Gannon made a sound and I froze. The air between us crackled with *something* and my eyes slowly made their way up to his.

My gaze was met with hot interest and curious desire. One slight movement would have brought our lips together, but neither of us moved. I longed to kiss him. Wanted him to drop his lips to mine. Instead, we stared at each other, the heat building, until the bell over the door chimed.

With the spell broken, Gannon cleared his throat and stepped away. "Yeah, these are good." He pulled the curtain closed as I went to see who had come in.

Gannon met me in the front of the store just as another shopper walked in.

"Good morning, welcome to Saint Nick's Heart," I said to the young mom with a toddler on her hip, and a little boy about five holding her hand. "How can I help you?"

The woman blushed. "Um, I was wondering if you had a coat in his size for cheap. He's grown out of it, but I was hoping to hand it down to his sister instead of trading it in. Maybe something around ten dollars?"

The scene that played out before me was definitely out of a holiday movie. Gannon tossed the coat and boots behind the counter and moved to stand next to me, his warm hand on the small of my back sending my brain, heart, and dick into a frenzy.

"I think we can do better than that," he said, his voice a mix of all-business and compassion like I'd never heard. "How about we get him a nice coat, we'll take the one that's too small, and get sister one just for her?"

The mom's eyes well with tears. "That's very kind of you, but I can't pay for two coats right now. She can wear his old one."

"Not a problem," Gannon said, taking over the transaction as if he'd lived and worked here his entire life, doing exactly what I would have done in the situation. "We've probably got the perfect coat for both kids and we'll take the old one as a trade."

The little boy tugged on his mom's arm. "Ciera would like a new coat, Mommy. She probably wants a pink one, not my old blue one."

The young woman nodded and brushed away a tear. "You're right, baby." She turned to us. "That would be so wonderful. Thank you."

"Okay, let's get some coats," Gannon said, clapping his hands together like he was truly excited for the challenge of finding these kids the perfect coats. I immediately missed the warmth of his hand on my back. "Mom, we've got some adult sizes over here for just seven dollars. Gently used, but great condition. If you're interested."

My heart nearly floated through the roof.

And I apparently had a bit of a thing for Gannon being all business-y and taking over. There was a very real chance I'd fail miserably if I had to keep my hands off him for very much longer.

He'd obviously noticed the mother wearing just a thin flannel and offered her the adult sizes at seven dollars as a way to help her. She'd said she needed something under ten dollars. We'd cover the kids' coats—hell, we could get her a coat for free as well—but Gannon seemed to understand the mom's need to purchase something even if she didn't have much to spend.

Thirty minutes later, Mom had picked out a nice coat, and both kids had coats they seemed very happy with. Gannon watched me as I rang up the sale and we both said goodbye as the little family headed out.

"Fuck," Gannon breathed out.

"What?"

"That was…" He paused, searching for the right word. "That was…a lot."

"A lot, how?"

"Good. It felt good. Sorry if I kinda just took over. Hell, I don't even know if those coats were seven dollars. I'll cover the difference. That baby probably wouldn't even have noticed she was wearing the brother's blue coat, but it just felt right for her to get a coat of her own, ya know?"

I smiled. "I know." Pressing my hip against his as we stood behind the register, I pushed my luck and let my pinky brush his hand. "The part of generous city slicker finding his place in the small holiday town will now be played by Gannon Snow."

Gannon took my hand and time stood still. "Damn, that felt good. Is it always like that? Feeling so good to help people?"

Not wanting to break the spell, wishing he'd hold my hand forever, I answered in a whisper, "Yeah, it always feels good, and we get to do it year-round."

"I think I never really understood why Joseph was so into helping people with this place, but I get it now." He squeezed my hand. Then, as if realizing he was holding my hand, he dropped it like he'd been burned. "Sorry," Gannon mumbled.

"Don't be," I said, turning toward him and leaving very little space between us. "Gannon, I—"

"Hayden, you here?" Dad called from the back.

Gannon jumped away from me like a teen caught in a compromising position.

"Yep!" I hollered back. "We're heading up the hill, just rang up an early-bird," I said, giving Dad and Mom hugs when they found us at the register. "Gannon, this is my mom and dad." Gesturing between the trio, I continued. "This is Gannon Snow, Joseph's grandson."

Despite knowing him for only a short time, I recognized the tension in Gannon's words when he stuck out his hand to shake. "Mr. and Mrs. Green, it's nice to meet you."

Mom batted his hand away and pulled him into a hug. "Gannon, it's so good to see you again. You probably don't remember us very well, but we always loved when you came to visit Joseph. He adored you and kept us all up-to-date on you over the years."

Gannon cleared his throat. "I do remember. This place was always good to me, I can see why Joseph was so enamored."

I knew Gannon felt terribly guilty about closing off his heart and not returning to St. Nicholas Crossing for such a long time. I understood the feelings, I really did, but I also knew that Joseph wasn't the type to hold a grudge and he'd just be thrilled his grandson had finally found his way to town—even if it took his death to get Gannon here.

Now, if only Gannon was willing to take his rightful place as a Snow in St. Nicholas Crossing. Maybe not taking over for Joseph, but continuing in his philanthropy.

"Well, I can tell you," Mom gushed, "Joseph would be so happy to have you here, God bless his soul. He always said his one wish—outside of keeping Saint Nick's Heart up and running to help people—was that you'd find your way here, find your way to a happy heart." She patted Gannon on the cheek. "We're sorry for your loss—Joseph will be missed terribly—but we're so happy to have you here. If you choose to stay, just know you'll be welcomed with open arms just the way Joseph would have wanted it."

I thought Gannon might have been close to grinding his teeth down to nubs if the clench of his jaw was anything to go by, so I stepped in. "We're heading up to the Snow place to go through Joseph's things. Dad, you good with us taking the old truck?"

"Sure thing," Dad said. "Now, keep in mind, it doesn't have the best heater and I wouldn't be taking it through any ice and snow on the steep roads, but it will get you to and from just fine without any surprise snowfall."

"Thanks."

Gannon cleared his throat. "Thank you both. And thank you for keeping this place running like Joseph would have wanted." Something like guilt crossed his face and he clenched his jaw again.

We said goodbye to my parents and headed over to the Ginger Snap Café.

"Well, well, well," Ginger teased. "Lookie here what the cat dragged in."

I gave her a hug before she bustled back behind the counter to take our orders. "Ginger, you remember Gannon Snow?"

"Of course, dear," she answered, genuine smile glowing on her face. "Gannon, we're glad to have you here. Anyone Joseph loved is always welcome."

I got the feeling Gannon was nearing the end of his rope with the compliments and reminders of his grandfather, so I ordered two of the breakfast sandwich specials and paid.

"You don't have to pay," Gannon grumbled.

"No big deal, my treat. Easier just to pay for the whole thing than try to split the order. You can get the next one."

Maybe by saying *the next one* I could make it come true.

Gannon winced. "God, that train. How are you not all walking around with blood pouring from your ears? Seriously, it's like nails on a chalkboard."

I cocked my head to listen. Sure enough, there was the

train whistle. I shrugged. "Just get used to it. Barely notice it."

"You're seriously telling me you didn't hear that until I pointed it out?"

"Seriously. When you're here long enough, it just becomes background noise you don't even notice."

Ginger came back with two bags, a cup of black coffee, and a cup of peppermint tea. "Where are you two off to today?"

"Heading up to the Snow place to do some sorting and organizing," I said, hoping Gannon didn't mind me taking over the conversation.

"Lucky for you, Joseph was very neat and tidy," Ginger said, her eyes taking on a fond look. "Gannon, when you have a moment, Candy and I would love to chat with you about your grandfather. He was a very special man and he loved you dearly—we'd love to share those stories."

Gannon stared at her for so long I thought maybe he hadn't heard her over the fading sound of the train—or maybe he was going to tell her no—but he finally nodded. "Hopefully before I head back to LA."

And there was another punch to the gut.

Not that I shouldn't have expected it, but it stung all the same.

We loaded up in the truck and dug into our food. The thick slices of Texas toast perfectly encased the eggs, cheese, bacon, and secret sauce of the sandwich and set my taste buds on fire. There was just enough kick throughout the slightly spicy, savory entrée.

"Damn, this is good," Gannon said around a mouthful. He dug back into the bag and pulled out a container I knew held the crispy goodness of home fries—perfectly fried, seasoned, and one of my very favorites from Miss Ginger's kitchen. "Damn," Gannon repeated around a bite of potatoes. "This food would be worth living here full time."

My heart caught in my chest. Damn, I wanted that. But I knew he was just saying the words—he'd never really stay in town just because of the food.

Maybe he'd be willing to stay for you.

I scoffed to myself and returned my focus on the road and my food. "Ginger is an amazing cook." I finished my home fries and stuffed the last bit of sandwich in my mouth, saving the pastry until we reached the top of the hill.

Putting the truck into a lower gear, I set to work navigating up the steep incline and sharp turns.

"Damn, a pastry too?" Gannon said. "She's selling these meals way too cheap."

"She does it because she loves to cook, loves to bring people together, and mostly just loves to help people. A homecooked meal for an affordable price is her gift to the people of Saint Nicholas Crossing."

Gannon just shook his head. "I didn't get it until earlier with those kids, but I do now. Look, I um…" He trailed off, clearly wanting to say something.

"You what?"

"I didn't know—didn't understand—how good it could be. But it feels like it's too late now."

Keeping my eyes on the road, but my attention turned to what Gannon was saying, I asked, "Too late for what?"

"I hadn't considered the good. Part of me wants to bask in all that goodness and never look back, but we both know I'm not long for this place. I'd drive people batty."

Even as Gannon said the words, I got the feeling he wanted me to protest—to say he'd never drive people up a wall and he'd be welcome here. Forever. The words would be true, but I wasn't sure it was the time or place to say them.

Gannon went on. "I'd be itching to leave and finding reasons to shut the shop down and fly back to LA."

"Shut the shop down?" I asked, my voice an octave higher as I pulled in at Joseph Snow's place. "Why? What are you talking about?"

Gannon studied me for a moment and then spoke as if I was a scared, trapped animal. "Hayden," he said, soft and slow. "Why do you think I'm here?"

I shrugged. "To go through your grandfather's stuff and get things organized, pay tribute to him, make an appearance in the town he loved so much. Probably sell his house."

Gannon nodded. "All of that is true." He grimaced. "But I came here to sell the store too."

"What? You can't do that," I said, scoffing at the notion as I climbed out of the truck, my boots crunching on the cold gravel of the driveway.

It was Gannon's turn to scoff. "It belongs to me, I can pretty much do anything I deem necessary."

My eyes bugged out. "And you *deem* it necessary to close down the heart of the only town your grandfather ever called home?"

Gannon stood tall, crossing his arms over his chest with an exasperated look on his face. "What else do you think I'd do with it? Stay here? Settle down? Take over for Joseph?" He huffed out a humorless laugh and began to pace. "Except for the last name, what in the world do I have in common with that man?"

"Oh, I don't know," I shot back, gesturing toward town. "Maybe under all that icy aloofness there's an actual heart. You know, a type of guy who would help out a mom and her two kids."

Gannon looked pained. "That was great and it really struck something in me. But can you imagine me here for the long haul? What a joke."

Cocking my head, studying his drawn face and realizing he was serious, I softened a bit. "Yeah, I can imagine you here for the long haul. And not just for selfish reasons." Not stopping at Gannon's brief look of shock and desire, I continued, "I get that we just met and it's kinda crazy to feel this way, but it feels like I know you. Feels like I know you more than some of the people around here I've known my whole life. You wouldn't be replacing Joseph. You'd be here as Gannon—but you've got that giving spirit, the generosity and willingness to help—"

Gannon scoffed.

"I'm serious. It may be hard to see because you've worked so hard at covering it up, but it's there." I frowned as I took in the gorgeous man in front of me. "And I don't think you've been trying to cover your generosity, it just got buried because you were so damn busy covering up your feelings. You didn't want to feel the bad, so you covered them all— including the good—in order to protect yourself. But the moment you stepped foot in this town—and I'm not even gonna mention the Christmas magic—you connected with the place, with your grandpa, and bits and pieces started to thaw."

"I've been here three days, it's not possible to feel this way toward a place—toward people—" His eyes caught mine and I gave in to the hope that he felt the same draw toward me that I felt toward him. "—so quickly. It's too much, too fast."

"And yet..." I stepped closer. "You can't stop the way you feel. I guess you can try—you've been doing it forever—but there's no getting around the natural draw of a place."

"My life is in LA," Gannon protested.

"I'm sure you miss it."

"I..." he said, wrinkling his brow, thinking, gauging his response. "I don't really miss any of it. But I've lived there my entire adult life—hell, even before I was an adult—I wouldn't know what to do anywhere else."

"You miss your apartment? Car? Friends? Favorite restaurants?"

Gannon stared off down the hill, shaking his head as if to clear the fog. "My apartment is fine. It's really nice. But I don't miss it. Don't have a car, just use a service. No real friends—except Ellen and she doesn't even live close, we just talk on the phone and video conferencing. Restaurants out there are great—tons of choices—but the unique ones seem to be trying too hard and the fancy ones are off the charts pretentious."

"The weather?"

He shrugged. "Weather is great. Smog sucks. Haven't had a breath of fresh air in decades. And it's so damn crowded." He spoke as if he'd traveled to LA in his head and stood in the middle of the city cataloging all the negatives. "Kinda like it though, no one pays much attention to you out there. Definitely no hugs or smiles from people you barely know."

I chuckled. "Sorry, Mom's a hugger."

"What would I even do here?" Gannon mused.

"We've got great internet. Do you have to be onsite to run your business?" I knew I was trying to sway him, but damn, I wanted Gannon to stay around. And knowing he thought he was in town to sell The Heart meant I had extra reasons to get him to stay.

"The business pretty much runs itself these days. I've got a great team working for me and Ellen handles a vast majority of it." He turned and stared at his late grandfather's house. "I can't even imagine just sitting here wasting away as I listened to that damn train hour after hour, day after day, year after year."

"I can't imagine that either," I scoffed. "Real estate is a prime business, right? Start something new here. Don't a lot of agencies spread out? You're one of the best—or that's what I'd guess—you could probably get something really good set up." I stood next to him and looked at Joseph's house. "The house is yours—it'll keep you busy for a while I'm guessing. Either get it ready to sell or make it a home." I cleared my throat, unsure of how Gannon would take my next words. "And, um, I'm not sure if you read everything regarding the shop…"

He turned to me. "What? What do you mean?"

"Um…Joseph left the store in our hands for the next year or so. This Christmas and next. Said if we could sustain it— keep it going as successfully as it's been—he'd make sure it belonged to the town."

Gannon grunted and rolled his eyes. "A shop can't belong to a town. Someone would have to be named as owner. I'm his only living heir, The Heart would become mine."

I chewed on my lip. "I saw the papers. I think you'd be named owner, but he had some sort of provision in there that the store couldn't be sold before this Christmas and next, and if a profit equal to or more than an average from the last five years of profits was made both years, the paperwork indicated you'd still be the owner, but the shop couldn't close or be sold." Unsure of myself because I knew fuck-all compared to what Gannon knew, I glanced at him in hopes he wasn't too pissed.

Gannon blinked at me slowly. "That's not possible…"

"What did the paperwork that you saw say? Surely it had to be the same, right? Joseph had a lawyer here and everything when the papers were signed."

He continued to blink at me and then he frowned. "Fuck."

"What?"

Gannon ran a hand through his hair. "I didn't actually read through the papers. *Fuck*."

Hope surged through me. The Heart was safe.

My heart, on the other hand, was likely on its way to obliteration at the hands of the man standing before me.

"Damn it," Gannon muttered. "Can we get inside and try to get warmed up? I've got a shit ton of work to do and I feel like a fucking idiot."

Taking pity on him, I nodded. "Yeah, grab your bag. Can you carry one of the heaters? I'll get the rest of our food and drinks."

We made our way up the steps to the massive wrap-around porch where Gannon reached into the mailbox for the key. "Can't believe he just left a key like this. Was always something that just amazed me when I was a kid."

"No one around here would steal from Joseph Snow and no one else would even know the place existed."

Gannon unlocked the door and we walked into the dimly lit house, setting down the larger items near the entry and moving farther into the little parlor area that opened onto a grand living room.

The only light streamed from behind the blinds and dust motes floated through the air with our disturbing arrival. The place smelled a bit musty, like it needed a good blast of fresh air, but it looked exactly as it had all the times I'd visited—almost as if Joseph had just gone to get us tea and would be right back.

"Fuck," Gannon whispered, shifting his bag on his shoulder.

I wasn't sure if he was cursing over the train whistle sounding in the background or over seeing his grandfather's house after such a long time away—or both—but I stepped closer. "Do you want to do this by yourself? I can leave and come back for you later." As badly as I wanted to stay by his side—like my heart had decided it beat more efficiently when we were together—I didn't want to make him uncomfortable.

Shocking the shit out of me—and probably himself—

Gannon reached out and grasped my hand. "No," he said, the word ragged as he gripped my fingers. "Stay. I hate everything I'm feeling, but my gut says I'd hate it even more if I were here alone."

As much as I wanted to let my heart soar at his words, I grounded myself with the knowledge Gannon just didn't want to be left alone with his emotions in his dead grandfather's house. It wasn't that he wanted *me* there.

"Oh my god, I'm such an asshole," Gannon bit out.

"What? Why?"

"He wanted to be cremated, right?"

I nodded.

"I haven't even asked about his ashes. Who has them?"

Smiling, I gave his hand a squeeze. "There's a tiny urn at The Heart for people to pay their respects. Ginger and Candy have one as well."

Gannon's brow quirked at that.

"And he wanted one left here," I said, pointing to the shelf over the fireplace. "For when you got here."

Gannon dropped my hand and his bag and walked to the fireplace. "He left a card?" he asked, picking up the small card in a sealed envelope.

"He left it with his lawyer around the same time as the papers were drawn up," I explained. "I think he had a feeling he wouldn't be with us much longer and he wanted things to be as settled and easy as possible."

"And I couldn't even get myself here for the funeral," Gannon rasped out.

"There was no funeral, just the way he wanted it. No ceremony or gathering of any type. Joseph wasn't a showy man. He wanted to be cremated and have The Heart live on, simple as that."

Gannon ran his finger along the edge of the card and stared at it before walking it to his bag and shoving it in a side pocket. He yanked his computer out and plopped down on the couch. "Internet work up here?"

I nodded. "Yeah, better even than in town somehow. Why?"

He tapped around on the keyboard. "Doing what I should have done when the papers were sent to me." Gannon clicked and scrolled, scowling, his lips moving silently as he read something. "Fuck."

"What?" Although, I knew what he'd discovered.

"The old man used to tell me he dreamed of me coming to live here and taking over the store for him—back then, it wasn't much, but it had already started to morph into what it is today—and I used to think that would be the greatest thing ever."

Gannon ran a shaky hand through his hair and sighed. "Used to wish I could live here full time and be away from my parents and their constant fighting, the way they used me against each other, the toxic, narcissistic behavior. I'd move here, live with Grandpa forever, and never look back. Back then, the thought of taking over the little store with him was something I wanted so badly."

He shook his head, lost in his memories. "Then my teen years hit, hormones overtook me, everything seemed to get harder, and I started realizing I could avoid feeling the bad shit in my life if I just blocked it all out. Scoffed off Grandpa's requests to come visit. Forgot all about the store. Threw myself into school with two goals in mind. One, money and success, because those made everyone happy, right? Two, shut it all down. Don't give into the sadness, anger, hurt, and loss over my parents being two of the worst humans in history. Don't remember the good with Joseph because it opened me up to the bad from all the rest."

Gannon leaned forward on his elbows and held his head in his hands. "He never stopped hoping I'd come back here.

Never stopped telling me how much he loved me and wanted me here, wanted me to take over The Heart. What used to be a dream as a child turned into kinda a joke in my adult mind. I was a rich, successful real estate agent and business owner. What in the hell would I do in Saint Nicholas Crossing? I laughed it off every time he brought it up in the cards or texts or rare phone calls." He pinched the bridge of his nose. "But he got me in the end. At least for a while. And I'm so damn high and mighty I didn't even take the time to read through the paperwork. You get two Christmases to make The Heart work, with or without me here. If you're successful, I can't sell. If not, I can do what I wish with the store." He sighed. "Fuck. What the hell am I going to do now?"

"Stay for a while? Let us show you how good The Heart is for people? Help us make it even better?"

Gannon stared at me as if not comprehending my words.

I shrugged. "Or go back to LA and let us do what we do best. We'd love to have you here, but we can do this on our own. You have to do what you think is best for you."

"I don't know that I can," Gannon answered raggedly.

"Which one?"

"Either? Both? I don't have an answer." He stood abruptly, pacing with his hands clenched in his hair.

"Hey," I said softly, touching his arm as he walked by.

Gannon jerked to a stop and glanced at my hand on his arm as if he'd forgotten I was even there.

"You came here to sort and organize. Give yourself the week at least. If you decide to stay longer, I'm sure you'll need to go back to LA to get clothes and make plans for being gone longer." I winked. "You strike me as the type who's used to traveling, maybe you can go back and forth for a while if needed. But you don't have to make all the decisions right now."

Gannon stared at me, blinking slowly, looking like he had trouble processing my words. "But why?"

"Why?"

"Why is it even a decision? It should be a no-brainer. Come in, do what I need to do, and leave. Done. Even with this ridiculous two-year plan with the store, I have no real reason to be here. This place has been fine without me, I'm not needed here. So *why* am I so torn? Why does part of me want to run screaming away back to LA and part of me thinks building a fire and celebrating Christmas in this damn tiny little town sounds just swell?" His voice had taken on a slightly panicked edge.

Squeezing his arm in hopes of grounding him a bit, I said, "First, there's a difference between being *needed* somewhere and *wanted*. Maybe we don't *need* you to make The Heart a success—you're right, we've been doing that for some time now and we're pretty damn good at it—but that doesn't mean you're not wanted here. And, even though you don't want to believe it, I'm a firm believer in…no, I'm not even going to chalk it up to magic since you'll scoff that off…I'm a believer in things working out the way the universe wants them to. Maybe neither of us realizes it just yet, but there's a reason you're here. Beyond the shop and the house, beyond finding closure with your grandpa. I truly believe there's something bigger at play. Maybe it's because that mom and her kids needed you. Maybe it's something you'll do later on that sets a whole miracle into motion. So, stop thinking you're not needed in some way and wanted in even more ways."

Gannon reached up and brushed a wayward chunk of hair from my forehead, his eyes going soft like maybe his heart was doing the same crazy flip-flop thing mine was. "Yeah, okay. I'll give it the week. Stick to my plan of heading out when I'm done here. I can always come back if needed."

My stomach plummeted at the thought of losing him when I'd just found him—or he'd just found me...or the universe had just shoved us together and told the magic to do its thing—but at least he'd calmed down a bit.

"Good plan. Let's get things set up here and get busy."

We flung open blinds and opened every single window before snacking on our pastries and finishing off our drinks while the house aired out—and Gannon bitched about being cold.

"We're bundled up," I said. "The more you're in it, the more used to it you'll get—but it's important to have the right gear."

Once we'd closed the windows—it hadn't taken long, but the icy breeze truly had freshened the place up and cleared the stagnant air nicely—I plugged in the heaters and sighed with relief to find the electricity was still on despite the gas for heat being turned off after Joseph died.

"So, I'm thinking we move the heaters to whichever room we're in and keep the doors closed since we don't want to try to heat the whole house," I said.

"Good idea." Gannon glanced at the fridge. "Should have thought ahead and brought some food if we're going to be up here for a bit."

"No worries," I said, hurrying over to my bag and pulling out two grocery sacks. "I figured I didn't need much in way of clothing, so I stocked other things." Smiling at Gannon's look of disbelief, I placed the bags on the counter. "It's not much and won't get us through a whole week, but I've got essentials." Not that *I* would be there a week, but I didn't bring that up.

Digging through the bags, I produced four huge deli sandwiches I'd picked up at Ginger's, granola protein bars, milk, a jug of water, loaf of bread, several cans of soup, a block of cheese, pretzels, and apples.

"Damn, no wonder you looked like you were about to tip over carrying that damn bag," Gannon teased. "Who knew you'd stuffed the whole store in there?"

I laughed and shrugged. "Figured we'd get hungry so I grabbed things that made sense." Pointing to the open pantry, I said, "And I had a feeling Joseph would have a few staples as well." The shelves were lined with gallon jugs of water along with a few shelf-stable canned and boxed goods. "He was always prepared since he could get stuck up here without much notice."

"At least we won't starve," Gannon said, then turned wide eyes my way. "I mean, I won't. I know you have to head back —I don't want to keep you from what you need to do."

I waved him away, despite wishing he'd ask me to stay— I'd arrange for a sub no problem if it meant more time with this man my heart had decided was *it* for me. Ridiculous, I knew, but there was no telling a heart what to do. "Let's get this stuff put away and get started."

Once the groceries were in the pantry, Gannon and I moved from room to room pulling the thick, heavy blinds in order to insulate the inside from the dropping temperatures outside. For its age, the house was well-insulated, but the blinds and curtains had been chosen specifically to help keep out the cold—and to keep the cool air inside during the warmer months.

"Since we've got electricity for the lights, it makes the most sense to block out the cold the best we can." I gestured toward the covered windows. "Where do you think we should start?" I asked.

Gannon stood with his hands on his hips and glanced around the house. "His office? Or do little things in each room? I'm guessing his office will take the most time."

"Let's do a room-by-room check and make note of what needs done. I know Candy and Ginger led a team in clearing a lot of stuff out upon his death—" I held up a hand when Gannon looked irritated. "All at his written wishes." When he was pacified, I went on. "But I'm sure each room has a little something to get to. And then you can focus on the office and set your own pace without the thought of other rooms looming over you."

Gannon took a deep breath and gave a weak smile. "Yeah, sounds like a plan. Let's get to work. The sooner we get started, the sooner this is finished."

I knew he meant going through the house, but I couldn't help the distraught feeling in my heart at the thought of whatever might be brewing between us being *finished* before it ever really even got started.

CHAPTER 7

Gannon

MY GRANDFATHER HAD BEEN a neat-nick for the most part. Probably because anything extra he had went to those in need, but I wasn't complaining because it meant there was less for me to sort through.

The fact Candy and Ginger had followed his wishes and cleared out so much of the house helped a lot too, even if I was slightly bent they'd gotten to do the job instead of me.

And how crazy was that? I didn't *want* the extra work and emotional upheaval, but I was slightly jealous of the women for being so close to my grandfather—closer than I'd been in several years.

Not to mention, the curiosity over their relationship was an itch I definitely wanted to scratch. Of course, as a child and preteen, I'd had no inkling my grandpa might have been involved in a polyamorous relationship. But as an adult, I'd worked a few things out in my head and realized Joseph had a life outside of being my grandfather.

I wanted to hear stories from Ginger and Candy, but I also wasn't sure my heart was ready for it.

And what was up with that? My heart had been firmly

protected behind an icy wall for years and years. Then I showed up with all my plans in this freezing-cold little Christmas town and all of a sudden the protective wall was melting and my heart decided it wanted to start feeling things?

No, thank you. I'd pass.

Snorting at myself, knowing my heart was definitely out to tear down the façade I'd worked so hard for all those years, I glanced across the kitchen at Hayden as he sorted through cabinets. Most of the non-perishables would go to the food pantry section of The Heart. Ginger and Candy had left all of that for me, knowing I'd likely need food while I was here, but I'd told Hayden we'd give the majority of it to people who needed it more than me.

The grin he'd given me had done weird things to my stomach. Like he was proud of me, like he believed in me. And suddenly, all I wanted was to get that happy little grin all the time.

I was beyond grateful for his help—the kid was generous to a fault and I got the feeling he stayed cheerful and busy, always giving to others, in an effort to take the spotlight off of his loneliness.

And damn, did I understand the loneliness when I actually allowed myself to think about it.

Hayden was a good worker—even if he whistled along with annoying holiday music he insisted on blasting from his phone as we worked—and I'd be lying if I said I wished he wasn't there with me.

But thank god he wasn't staying.

Because I didn't know how much longer I could keep my hands to myself.

All I wanted to do was shut the two of us in a room with a fire or a heater, strip him naked, and spend hours exploring his body. Everything about the man had me on edge—in a good way. Those navy-blue eyes, that gorgeous russet-colored hair that seemed to have a mind of its own, the pale skin tinged with freckles, and that perfect ass he couldn't keep hidden no matter which pants he wore.

Luckily, since we were working, he wasn't wearing the suspenders and bowtie because I'd developed quite the fantasy of him in nothing but a jock, the tie, and suspenders as he rode me.

That shit needed to vacate my brain immediately.

I wanted him like no man I'd wanted before.

He wasn't more attractive than any of the men I'd been with—but he definitely had a very different look than the guys I'd usually found myself fucking. Hayden was just unique—so opposite of most guys I'd been with—and I felt drawn to him like no other.

Yes, I wanted him in my bed. Under me, on me, anyway I could get him, but there was more to it—and that was the part throwing me for a loop.

Wanting more with a guy wasn't my usual M.O.

See a hot guy, fuck him, maybe keep him around for as long as the sex was good and the relationship benefitted us both, say goodbye, and start it all over again.

That was what I did.

Then I found myself in St. Nicholas Crossing with a guy pretty much the complete opposite of anyone I'd ever been with and all I could think about—outside of railing him into the mattress—was getting to know him better, watching movies with him, surprising him with a gift to a spa to force him into taking time for himself, and building something with him.

And what the actual fuck was that?

It didn't help that Hayden was flirty and touchy and I kept catching looks on his face that indicated he'd be very much down with bedroom activities and *more*.

The bedroom activities weren't an issue.

We had a week and I had zero problem with a quick little holiday fling.

But I'd already established my heart was completely out of whack in St. Nick's Crossing and I wasn't confident I'd be capable of keeping it under control if the sex potentially turned into something more.

Fuck.

Since when did I ever worry about sex turning into something more?

Since you met Hayden and got all melty over his eyes and his smile.

I huffed and shoved unneeded kitchen towels into a donation bag.

Just ask him if he wants to fuck around—keep it casual. He knows you're leaving.

My gut clenched.

See, that was the problem.

I had every intention of leaving and never looking back.

Except…

Everything in me argued that I should stay.

Especially if Hayden and I started something.

I had this feeling if I ever got to touch him, hold him, slide into his tight heat, I'd never want to let him go.

And that was a problem.

So, my options were:

Me and my right hand for the rest of the week. Leave this place. Move on with my life. Do my best not to wonder what might have been. Forget Hayden and all the warm, swirly feelings he and St. Nicholas Crossing had stirred in me.

Or…

Take him to bed. Have a fun week of hot, sweaty sex. Leave this place. Move on with my life. Have a handful of great memories to look back on. Wish Hayden the best and forget all the warm, swirly feelings he and St. Nicholas Crossing had stirred in me.

Or…

Fuck him senseless. Stick around. Get to know him. Take him on dates like my heart was screaming to do. Give in to the warm, swirly feelings churning at my core. And see if Hayden's theory about the universe putting me exactly where it wanted me had any merit.

Or…

Fuck.

I could have gone on and on with the scenarios and I had no idea which was the right thing to do.

If I stayed, I couldn't imagine myself here for life.

Right?

Would Hayden and I have something great until I got the itch to return to LA?

Then what?

Heartache and loneliness all over again?

Could I do that to Hayden?

To myself?

The fucking train shrieked through town and jerked me from my thoughts. For once, I was almost grateful for the damn thing because I wasn't sure I wanted to stay trapped in my head with all the fucked up thoughts and indecision.

I didn't *do* indecision.

I was a fucking top-notch, successful businessman.

I made a plan and executed it.

If the plan had to be adjusted based on unexpected circumstances or a change in the situation, I pivoted and made executive decisions before carrying out the plan.

I didn't hem-haw around like a damn angsty teen trying to decide if I should tell my crush I wanted to kiss him.

Wanted to do so much more than kiss him.

Yet, there I was, stuck in Christmas Town Hell with the

most mesmerizing, sexy, cute man I'd ever met, waffling back and forth like a damn fucking teeter-totter.

"So, tell me about LA. You live all high and mighty? Hot guys, fancy dates, lifestyles of the rich and famous?" Hayden asked, a mischievous twinkle in his eyes.

I eyed him suspiciously as we headed to the living room, sliding the old doors closed to shut off the room from the rest of the house so the heaters could do their job. I didn't plan on us being in there long, there were only a couple chests, a bookshelf, and something I would have called an armoire to go through.

"Hold that thought," Hayden said, standing in the middle of the living room. "Am I the only one who just noticed there's no furniture in here?"

I glanced around and shrugged. "Guess I hadn't really noticed, but it makes sense if they took it down to The Heart. Not like anyone's been here to use the couch and chairs."

Hayden nodded. "True, just shocked I hadn't noticed it. Okay," he gestured toward me, "carry on with the story."

"What story?" I asked with a smile.

"The one you were going to entertain me with so I can live vicariously through you. About all of your steamy dates and fancy dinners."

Chuckling, I opened a chest and began sifting through the contents. "I think you'll be sorely disappointed."

Hayden scoffed. "Don't act like you didn't have guys hanging off you, begging for you to take them to bed after swanky dinners and high-priced drinks at exclusive clubs."

I cocked my head. "Okay, maybe, but it wasn't all that great if I'm being honest."

"Mmhm," Hayden hummed. "Please, tell me how dreadful your high-end lifestyle was. Unload about your empty love life," he teased.

Pausing, my hands running over the soft quilt Grandpa

always let me sleep with when I came to visit—memories of better times barreling over me—I shook my head. "Not to get all dramatic, but every part of my life out there truly was empty and meaningless."

God, now this place had me all reflective and maudlin.

Hayden raised a brow.

"I count Ellen as a friend. Everyone else I had any contact with would be categorized as either a business acquaintance, colleague, or meaningless hookup."

"You didn't have any long-term relationships?"

I snorted. "Longest I kept a guy around was a couple months."

"Why?"

Shrugging, I set the quilt aside—I was keeping it for sentimental reasons even though I didn't *do* sentimental—and continued digging in the chest. "The only thing most of the guys I ever dated had in common with me was sex. They liked my money. Liked that I had connections. Liked that we looked good together. Outside of that, they were usually snooty, materialistic, gold-diggers just looking for someone to fund their spending habits and set them up for a cushy future."

Hayden wrinkled his brow. "God, that sounds horrible. How'd you keep finding guys like that?"

"More like they found me," I said before grimacing. "That sounds bad. I don't mean all these guys were chasing me, I just mean I wasn't looking for them. I didn't have any interest in a relationship."

"Why?"

Nosy little shit.

"Just never felt it."

"Weren't you lonely?" Hayden asked softly.

I nodded. "Yeah, not that I ever would have admitted it out there. But it feels okay to tell you for some reason.

Loneliness was a constant—even when I had a man in my life for a few days or a couple months—but I learned to cover it all up, just like I blocked out everything else."

"So, you stuck with meaningless men you'd never want anything real with so you'd be able to keep yourself completely detached, even though it meant you never felt connected or wanted or loved."

I huffed and closed the now-empty chest—I had serious thoughts about keeping Grandpa's chests for myself. "Sounds about right."

"That's sad."

"Maybe, but it kept me from feeling anything. I had no interest in any kind of meaningful conversation with people out there—these few days with you? Most I've talked outside of business shit in…well, probably in over ten years." I gave him a wry smile. "Guess this damn place has me feeling all talkative. May be the company too."

Hayden bit his lip and I had to turn away to keep from groaning out loud.

"What about you? Tell me about the guys you've dated."

"Ha," Hayden bit out. "It's not like there are a lot of choices around here. Thought I'd do better in the city, but I was homesick and felt so out of place. The men I dated didn't get me. The ones who wanted a bad boy said I was too soft, too nice. The ones who wanted arm candy said I was too small-town. The ones who just wanted sex said I got too attached." He huffed and tried to laugh it off, but I caught the tear glinting in his eye. "That's me, too much and never enough. At least here, I know I make a difference." He turned from me and I watched his shoulders rise and fall with a deep, calming breath.

Without giving it a second thought, I stood from my place on the floor and stalked toward Hayden. Gripping his shoulders, I spun him around to face me and tipped his chin up to meet my eyes. "I need you to hear me and make no mistake. You. Are. Enough. You're the most kindhearted, generous, caring man I've ever met. You must be some kind of miracle worker to have me chatting like a damn magpie— never felt as comfortable around someone as I do around you. You aren't too much. Not too soft, too nice, too small-town."

Hayden's eyes, shining brightly with tears, caught mine and he licked his lips. "Yeah? You really think so?"

"I think being treated nicely by you has been the best thing I've experienced in years. I think your small-town ways are charming." I ran a thumb over his lips. "I think I've dreamed about your softness ever since meeting you and I'd give anything to feel it against me, savor it, explore every soft inch of your body," I whispered gruffly.

Fuck.

But I didn't have time to worry about my words, because Hayden whimpered and trembled under my hands and I had no choice but to pull him close and bring my lips down on his.

Hayden tasted like peppermint, his soft lips yielding to mine as he accepted the slip of my tongue. One of us groaned and his arms came up around my neck as my hand held the back of his head and tilted his head for better access to his delicious mouth.

His soft scent of mint, balsam, and grapefruit surrounded me, teasing my senses, and making me want to pour myself into him.

But Hayden's frustrated little groans of pleasure as he rocked against me grounded me and had me pulling back from the hottest, sexiest kiss of my entire life.

No, it hadn't been the smoothest or most practiced, but claiming Hayden's mouth as mine after wanting to have him in my arms since the moment I'd laid eyes on him had been everything I'd hoped for and more.

And I'd pulled away.

I sighed and pressed my forehead to his as we both caught our breath.

"Why'd you stop?" Hayden asked, his pretty mouth drawn into a tiny pout.

Running a hand through my hair, I huffed out a humorless laugh. "Figure we've got some time. No need to rush. We're still here to get a job done."

"Was it not good?" Hayden asked.

I ran a thumb over his kiss-swollen lips. "Kissing you was the best thing I've done in years. But if I let things go further now, we'll never get any work done."

"So, you want to do more?" Hayden asked, his cheeks flushed and eyes hopeful.

"Fuck. Yes."

He bit his lip—almost bringing me right back to wanting to kiss him for the rest of my life and forget about what we came here to do—and bounced on his toes. "Okay. I want that too, just so you know. Consent and all that."

I groaned and wondered just what type of trouble this man would get me into.

We made our way to the spare room, the last one we needed to work on before moving to the office, and Hayden twirled around in the middle of the vast room. "Good thing I'm not staying," he said.

"Why?" I knew it *was* good he wasn't staying—on the surface—because I'd only want to tumble him into bed and fuck him senseless, but it kinda hurt to hear him say it.

"No couch, no spare bed, we'd have to play out the *there's only one bed* trope," Hayden said with a wicked grin.

For the first time since walking into the room, I noticed the bed was gone. Joseph really had given away the majority of his house. Honestly, though, I understood it. Wasn't like he could use them and he knew others needed them more. He'd left some of what he thought I might want and I appreciated that.

The room warmed up quickly with the heaters and closed doors. I ignored the thought of sharing a bed with Hayden, and we worked alongside each other with only a tiny bit of awkwardness—mostly from the fact I wanted to say fuck it and take him to bed, that kiss replaying on a steamy loop in my head.

"You know I'm going to have to show you just how good Saint Nick's Heart can be so you won't be able to bring yourself to sell it, right?" Hayden asked, a wry smile on his face as he boxed up miscellaneous items I handed to him.

I had to smile. "I wouldn't expect anything less."

"Good," Hayden said. "You've seen it in action, you know deep down that it's the heart of the town, the reason so many families make it through the year, but I'm going to make sure you know it has to keep running."

Shaking my head and chuckling, I kept going through the items on the closet shelf. "It's got to make as much or more profit as it's made in the last five years for me to even consider keeping it—and that's based on the paperwork straight from Joseph. It can't be a decision made just on *feeling* like the store does a good thing. And it's a business—not just a charity—so we're not keeping it going if it's not bringing in money."

"You don't care that it keeps people from being cold or hungry?" Hayden narrowed his eyes. "All you care about is the money?"

I shrugged. "I don't want people to be cold and hungry, but I'm also not going to pour money into a place that doesn't bring in a return."

He nodded. "I get that. And if it's not profiting, it won't

be around to help people for long whether you opt to sell it or not."

We finished up in the spare bedroom and I squirmed a bit under Hayden's scrutiny—I knew he was determined to keep The Heart and I knew he was irritated with me for not saying the store could stay in business even if it didn't make a profit both years.

But it didn't make sense to sink money or time into a place if it wasn't bringing in a return.

And if The Heart disappears? What about the town Joseph loved so much?

I pushed away the thoughts and went back to organizing.

"Just got the office left," I said, hoping to move beyond the bit of tension.

"Yeah," Hayden sighed. "You want me to stay or head on down the hill? I can take these boxes whenever you give the word."

I want you to stay I thought, but instead, I checked the time and I groaned. "You might as well head on down, I'll maybe get an hour or so done on the office, but I'll leave most of it for tomorrow. No need for you to be driving in the dark."

"I can stay, it's not a big deal." Hayden bit his lip and I wondered if he wanted to crawl into bed with me and not emerge until spring.

Or was that just me?

"As much as I'd like you to stay, it may be for the best if we didn't start something we can't finish," I said, kicking myself for turning away an eager and willing participant.

"Who says we can't finish?" Hayden asked, his head cocked to the side. "I told you, I'm on board with more of whatever that was earlier. I know the score. I know you're leaving. And I know whatever we'd start would end when you left."

It was my turn to cock my head. "And you're okay with that? A holiday fling? Just this week and nothing more?"

Hayden shrugged. "It's what I'm used to. It's what you do."

Ouch.

"Plus, who says I'm not keeping my fingers crossed for a round two if and when you come back from time to time?" Hayden winked. "And we better hope it's *good* before we get too far ahead of ourselves."

Oh, it would be good. I had no doubt of that when the sweet heat of that kiss still clung to my lips.

I groaned, wanting so damn badly for him to stay, but I was trying my best to make the right decision.

And who says sending him away, keeping him out of your bed, is the right decision?

"Head on home," I gritted out. "I may regret it—and I can't say I'll be able to avoid it forever—but it's probably best if you go on home."

Hayden's face fell and I wanted to pull him close, wrap him in my arms, and never let go.

But he just nodded. "Yeah, okay. See ya." He pressed his lips together. "I may be really into you, and god knows I'm desperate, but you won't hear me begging for your attention." He huffed out a wry chuckle. "I only beg if you make it worth my while," he said with a twinkly wink. "You can call the store and let whoever answers know you're ready when you need a ride back down."

He bent to pick up a stack of boxes and I followed him to the door.

"Thanks for all your help," I said, hoping I sounded genuine.

Hayden grunted and I opened the door.

A blast of cold, wet air slammed into me and Hayden stopped short.

"Holy shit," he breathed.

We both backed up. Hayden put down the boxes and I shoved the heavy door shut.

"What the fuck was that?" I asked.

"It's called snow. A type of precipitation that one might see in winter. It forms when tiny ice crystals in the clouds stick together and fall to the ground," Hayden deadpanned.

I rolled my eyes and elbowed him. "I *know* what snow is, smartass. I meant where the hell did a damn blizzard come from? There wasn't a cloud in the sky when we walked in here…" I paused to look at my watch, "shit, over eight hours ago."

"Damn, no wonder I'm hungry," Hayden joked. My unamused look sobered him up and he shrugged. "I told you, we get weird weather patterns around here. It's enough of a phenomenon that meteorologists have come to study the area. They've never come up with anything solid which is why townsfolk usually just chalk it up to holiday magic."

I scoffed.

Hayden gave me a look. "I get that you don't believe in it, but sometimes it's easier to put it on the magic than try to figure out the *why* behind something no one else seems to be able to explain. Without holiday magic we'd be forced to wonder if this place is cursed when a foot of snow falls unexpectedly."

My head jerked up from where I'd been holding it in my hands. "A *foot*?"

He shrugged again. "I didn't get much of a look at it, but it looked like about that."

"What do we do?" A slight panic coursed through me at the thought of the answer.

Hayden cocked a brow. "Well, I'm not equipped—or willing—to attempt a trek down the hill, so it looks like you're stuck with a roommate for a bit. Outside of that, we hope the electricity stays on—there's a generator in case it doesn't—and give thanks for heaters and blankets and food."

My blood pressure skyrocketed and my eyes bugged. "How long do you think we're stuck?"

Hayden shrugged. "No tellin', honestly. If it stops and then warms up with a lot of sun, things will melt pretty quickly. If it dumps much more or stays cloudy and colder, may be looking at about a week—assuming another system doesn't add to it." He gestured toward the general vicinity of outside. "Once it stops, the crew will set to work clearing streets and roads, but they won't start on the hill until the town is cleared—clearing the hill road is a bitch."

"So, we're just stuck here at the mercy of the weather and a crew of snowplow trucks?" I asked, feeling my irritation at things out of my control rising.

"No, we're stuck here at the mercy of the weather and a couple good Samaritans with snowplow blades on their trucks. The county doesn't help out much when it comes to clearing snow—they leave it mostly to us to take care of our own. We're used to it so it's no big deal."

I groaned and pinched the bridge of my nose. "Fuck."

"Hey, you planned to stay up here and work through Joseph's office anyway, right?"

I nodded.

"And you've got your bag, your laptop, chargers, all that. You can work through his stuff, take care of any work things. I'll do my best to stay out of your way," he said with a shrug. "Maybe look at this time as a vacation of sorts. Read, rest, enjoy your downtime. Sometimes the holiday magic gives us opportunities we didn't even know we needed."

The words he said made sense—except for the magic part—but all my brain—and cock—heard was, *"You're stuck with this gorgeous man. You've kissed him. You want so much more with him. You're going to have to share a damn bed with him. And your fucking heart is already way too much involved for this situation to go any direction but south.*"

"Do we have enough food?" I asked.

"We won't be eating like kings, but we won't starve. I brought stuff and Joseph had a few things in the pantry. We'll work through the perishables first and save the shelf-stable things for later. Plenty of water and we could always melt snow if needed. Would be nice if the gas was on so we'd have heat, but we've got the fireplaces in most of the main rooms and the heaters." Hayden placed a warm hand on my upper arm. "I know it's not ideal and you'd rather not be stuck here with me, but we're not in any danger."

Speak for yourself I thought. My heart was already on shaky ground. A damn blizzard and being stranded with Hayden was maybe just enough to send me over the edge.

CHAPTER 8
Hayden

I WATCHED panic fill Gannon's face. Whether from being snowed-in, the situation being out of his control, being stuck with *me*, or a variety of other potential reasons, the man was on edge.

"I'm going to take a look outside while you decide what to do with the office. Start tonight or leave it until tomorrow. I'll put together some food. After dinner, we can shower and watch a movie or something."

We were lucky the house still had electricity to run most of the house. Not having the gas on for heat sucked and—damn, with no heat we had no hot water. I frowned.

"What?" Gannon asked.

"Just thinking about hot water. The water heater is gas powered, I'm sure. We may have to heat our bath water." I pointed toward the basement door. "I'm going to check on things down there. Knowing Joseph, he had some sort of backup water heater—the man was always prepared."

Figuring Gannon needed a bit of time to himself to adjust to the idea of being stuck, I headed down to the basement.

Pulling the string on the single-bulb light hanging from the low ceiling, I glanced around.

Bingo.

A huge gas water heater sat to one side of the furnace.

But to the other side I spied a smaller electric water heater. I wasn't much of a handyman, but I knew the electric model would at least keep us with enough warm water for some short showers during our forced stay.

I flipped the switch, listened to it buzz to life, and headed back up the stairs.

The house was silent, the distant sound of a train whistle blowing through the howling wind of the nasty weather outside, and I made my way toward where I figured Gannon would be.

Sure enough, he was in Joseph's office.

"We're in luck," I said, but my words died on my lips.

Gannon stood with his hands bracing himself against a bookshelf, shoulders shuddering, pictures of him and Joseph in front of him.

Not caring that he'd probably tell me he wanted to be alone, I walked over to him and nudged my way between him and the shelf, wrapping my arms around him.

I got the distinct impression Gannon didn't have a lot of experience with hugs as an adult, but his tension eventually dissolved and he let me hold him.

He wasn't a blubbering mess—I had a feeling Gannon didn't blubber, not that I would have thought any less of him —but he was definitely caught up in missing his grandfather.

"It's okay to miss him," I said.

Gannon huffed. "It feels like I don't even have a right to miss him. I left and never looked back. He had whole relationships—with not one but *two* women from what I can tell—and friendships and connections with this town...all while I strutted around in LA like I was big stuff." He gestured toward the other pictures on the shelf—Joseph with Ginger and Candy, Joseph with my parents and me, Joseph with a bunch of kids, Joseph with a crew of friends—and took a deep breath. "Those people deserve to miss him. Those people were the ones there for him. Me? I ran away."

"Yeah, you did," I answered simply and Gannon stiffened. "But Joseph understood."

"He shouldn't have had to understand why his grandson was being an ass. I loved this place with every fiber of my being when I was a child. Idolized him." Gannon stepped away from the hug and paced the office. "Maybe it was because it hadn't gotten so bad yet, or maybe the good just still outweighed the bad when I was a kid, but then I went and got all fucked up thanks to my parents getting worse and worse, and shut it all out." He ran a frustrated hand through his hair. "Because *I* didn't want to feel the shitty side of things, Grandpa suffered. I don't deserve to be upset about his passing."

I grabbed his arm and whirled him around. "First, that's what I meant when I said Joseph understood. He didn't blame *you* for your actions—he blamed your parents. He hated what they did to you—maybe they didn't physically abuse you, but being subjected to their violent, toxic relationship was just as bad. Did he wish you'd figured out a way to avoid the hard emotions and still allowed yourself to feel the good and spend time with him here? Yes, but he didn't hold any of that against you."

Gannon started to pull away, but I held firm and barreled on.

"Second, you have every right to be upset about his passing. Doubly so, if you ask me. Not only are you mourning his death, you're mourning what could have been, mourning the years you missed out on. It's not a competition to see who misses him the most or who deserves to be the saddest over his death." My hand burned on his arm, but I didn't move it. "You're allowed to feel what you feel. You loved him. Being back here is stirring up a lot of emotions. Joseph would tell you to greet each one as if it were an old friend, sit with it a while, and decide if you'd like to invite it in or send it on its way."

Gannon stared at me for a bit and then chuckled. "Yeah, that sounds exactly like something he'd say." He glanced over at the pictures. "It's just a lot coming all at once and guilt is the heaviest one right now."

"Makes sense. But here's the thing, once you've sat with that guilt for a while, you need to realize it's not helping Joseph. He'd so much rather you do something good for the town than sit and wallow in guilt over not seeing him before he died."

Gannon nodded. "I get that. He was truly an amazing man."

"And he has an amazing grandson," I said softly, squeezing his arm before letting go.

Gannon's eyes met mine and, for a moment, I thought he was going to lean in and kiss me again. Instead, he just swallowed and moved away to absently shuffle a pile of papers on the desk.

"What did you mean when you said we're in luck?" he asked.

"Oh!" I took Gannon's attempt at changing the subject to something easier. "There's an electric water heater in addition to the gas one—like I said, Joseph was always prepared—so we'll have warm water."

"Perfect." Gannon glanced around the room. "I'm not going to start in here tonight."

"You go shower. I'll start dinner."

Gannon took my suggestion and thirty minutes later we

were settled in the little breakfast nook with dinner while the snow piled up outside.

Our soup and sandwiches weren't much, but I figured we'd be begging for something more than soup and pretzel sticks by the time we were able to leave the house.

"You should go take a nice long soak in the tub," Gannon said.

"What? No, I'm fine. I'll just clean up the—" I stopped abruptly when Gannon's strong hands landed on my shoulders.

"Hayden, you're constantly keeping yourself busy. Always taking care of others. You're damn amazing and people are so lucky to know your cheerful little elf helper self." He grinned when a giggle escaped my lips at his description. "But you deserve to take time for yourself as well. Take a book with you. Run the tub full with the hottest water you can stand. Pour in some bubbles if you find them. And relax for a bit." He gestured toward the heavy curtains blocking out much of the cold. "We're here for a while and you've already told me I should treat it like a vacation, so you can do the same."

My heart wiggled and squirmed in my chest at Gannon's words.

No man had ever cared enough about me to make me take time for myself.

Maybe that's because you dated assholes.

Or maybe because the couple hookups a year aren't around long enough to worry about you taking care of yourself.

I nodded. "Okay. You wanna watch a movie after?"

"We can, if I haven't already fallen asleep."

I froze. "Oh, um…"

Gannon chuckled. "Yeah, we've got our very own *there's only one bed* trope. No worries. If Vince and Kota could do it, I figure we'll survive."

His reference to the book I'd loaned him had me

wondering if he was thinking about what Vince and Kota got up to when they shared that bed.

Whether the steamy scene was on his mind or not, Gannon continued. "I'll make sure there are fresh sheets and we can put a pillow wall down the middle if it would make you feel better."

I scowled at him. "I think I proved earlier that I'm not interested in any pillow wall." I stood on my tiptoes and pressed a kiss to his cheek. "A snowed-in holiday fling sounds absolutely perfect to me."

Gannon groaned. "Go take a bath."

Smiling, I grabbed a heater and made my way to the bathroom.

It wasn't that I didn't do nice things for myself from time to time—and I truly did get enjoyment from helping and caring for others—but having Gannon notice and care enough to suggest I take a moment for myself was really nice.

And it did strange flip-floppy things to my heart.

Things I had no business feeling toward a guy I'd just told I was completely fine with having a holiday fling.

Fling meant short and easily ended.

He was leaving.

No matter how quickly I'd gotten used to him being here.

No matter how much my romantic-at-heart little brain wanted to imagine what life would be like if Gannon stayed forever.

He.

Was.

Leaving.

We could have our fun.

He'd go back to LA and we'd maybe hook up from time to time when he came to town to check on things.

Eventually, he'd bring someone with him—or if a miracle

occurred, maybe I'd have someone in my life—and we'd let the memories of what we used to have be enough.

I turned on the heater and rummaged through the closet for some bubble bath.

"Well, well," I murmured to myself. "What do we have here?"

Grinning like a loon, I pulled out a four-pack of enemas with only one missing.

Don't get me wrong, I knew enemas had functions outside of prepping for anal sex. But as a gay man who was very much onboard with the idea of sex with Gannon—and who didn't want to think about Joseph or Candy or Ginger needing enemas for *any* reason—I chose to look at this bundle-pack as a magical, wondrous gift from the holiday gods.

After a nice, long leisurely soak in some sort of wintery-scented bath oil, I took advantage of the rest of the hot water and sent a silent thank you to whoever had stocked the closet while I took care of a hopeful prepping. Maybe I was assuming too much, but I figured it was better to be prepared.

Gannon tossed his book to the side when I slipped into the toasty bedroom.

"You built a fire?" I asked, shivering at the chill of the house, grateful for the warm room. Wrapped in two towels, one around my waist and one around my shoulders like a shawl, I made my way to the corner of the room in hopes of finding something to sleep in without looking too much like I was totally coming onto Gannon.

I mean, I was fine with him tackling me to the bed and having his way with me, but being dressed in towels wasn't a seduction routine, just a necessity.

"I was surprised I remembered how," Gannon said,

looking pleased as punch with himself, his eyes skimming my body as he watched me curiously.

"Not that I doubt you, but you opened the damper?"

Gannon nodded. "I did. Even shone my flashlight up the chimney to make sure there was no debris. Looked like it had been cleaned recently. And some sort of mesh covering to keep birds out? Probably makes it difficult for Santa to shimmy on down, but I guess he figures out a way, huh?"

I pressed a hand to my chest. "Did Gannon Snow just indicate Santa was real?"

"Doesn't Santa go along with your holiday magic nonsense?" Gannon asked with a chuckle as I opened the wardrobe.

"Santa is folklore. Holiday magic is different. Now, don't get me wrong, they go together in many ways, but there are a lot of people who look at Santa as just a story and the magic as being very real." I rummaged around until I found a long-sleeve thermal shirt.

"What are you looking for?"

"Luckily, we didn't empty this out for donations yet."

"I guess I figured it would be the last one since I was staying in here. Why?"

"One of us brought an overnight bag for staying, while the other one of us filled his bag with groceries since he wasn't staying. I had a couple pair of underwear, socks, toiletries, and an extra prescription bottle left from the last time I spent the night somewhere, but no real clothes."

I could easily wear the clothes I'd had on that day for several more days, assuming I didn't get them dirty while sorting papers, but sleepwear was also needed.

"I can wash underwear as needed, but this will have to do for pajamas," I said, holding up the thermal shirt before losing my shawl-towel and yanking the thermal over my head.

Joseph had been a lot bigger than me, so the shirt fell to my knees. Which was good since I didn't want to waste underwear for sleeping. Unwrapping the towel from my waist, I hung it on the knob of the dresser before crawling into bed.

"Fuck," Gannon muttered. "That damn book."

"You don't like it?" I asked, rolling to my side, loving the soft rasp of clean sheets against my bare legs.

"I like it. Which annoys me. It's cute—kinda sappy. But it's also fuckin' hot and now I've got a sexy little elf going commando in my bed and I'm supposed to sleep?" Gannon threw an arm over his face. "If holiday magic exists, it's torturing me."

Giving him a suggestive smile, I edged a bit closer. "Does the thought of hooking up with me really cause you so much...whatever it's causing you?"

"Hesitation? Concern?"

"Not exactly words a guy wants to hear when it comes to thoughts of sex with him," I muttered.

"It would be one thing if I didn't know you. Or I was leaving tomorrow. Or we'd never see each other again. But we both have a connection to this town. We're entangled. And I might be leaving, but I'll be back at some point."

"And?"

Gannon huffed. "And part of me wants to say fuck it, but another part of me says sex with you would just screw with my head even more—make it harder to leave, or harder to stay away."

I reached over, under the covers, and placed my hand on Gannon's bare chest, loving the smattering of crisp hair there. Loving his sharp intake of breath even more. "No one says you have to leave—that's a you thing. And would it be so terrible if you didn't want to stay away?"

I knew I sounded a bit desperate.

I knew I didn't have the right to ask him to stay, or even hint at it.

If Gannon stayed, or if he came back, it had to be because it was what *he* wanted, not because I'd used the desire pulsing between us to coerce him.

Not that I thought Gannon Snow could be coerced, but the sexual tension between us was palpable and had me wondering when—not if—it would explode.

"I'm not saying no to whatever this is," Gannon said, his hand covering mine on his chest. "But let's sleep for now. We'll see how we feel about things in the morning."

He groaned.

"What's wrong?" I asked, suddenly concerned.

"That damn train."

I cocked my head. Sure enough, the whistle blasted to announce the train going through St. Nicholas Crossing. With a shrug and a grin, I said, "Honestly, stick around long enough and you won't even notice it."

"That might be reason enough to stay—fucking thing is like nails on a chalkboard."

I knew he was just griping, but my heart sank a bit.

As selfish and unfair as it was, *I* wanted to be reason enough for him to stay.

If I was being honest, letting things go further than a kiss between us was probably not the best idea.

Hot, sexy, and satisfying?

Yes.

Good for my heart to get even more involved and end up being shattered?

No.

Not at all.

But like a moth to a flame, I wanted the experience, even if it meant pain down the road. Despite the fact I knew it would hurt, I didn't want to one day regret the fact I'd never come apart under Gannon's touch.

I didn't understand the lightning-quick draw I'd had to this man. Didn't know why it felt as if I'd known him my whole life and was just waiting for him to come to his senses and love me.

Love me.

I'd never in my life thought I was in love.

It was absolutely crazy to think I might love a man I barely knew, but I'd felt infatuation and the feelings swirling in my gut, in my blood, were so much deeper. So much more. So very real.

The upheaval Gannon had brought to my heart and soul was scary and exciting, but I had this unexplainable feeling that it would all be worth it in the end.

If Gannon was on the same page.

I sighed and snuggled deeper into the soft, warm blankets.

With the day catching up to us and no real reason to keep talking, we eventually fell asleep with the wind howling outside.

I woke several hours later warm and toasty in Gannon's arms. Did the man know he was an A-plus cuddler? Or would he claim it was just from the cold?

The fire still glowed and the room was almost uncomfortably warm, so I'd call bullshit if he tried to say holding me close was just for warmth.

I knew the moment he woke to realize he had me tight in his arms. Gannon tensed and started to move away. "Sorry," he grumbled. "Don't usually maul my bed partners."

Gripping his arm to keep him close, I shifted closer to him. "So, it's just me you hold in your sleep? That's kinda cute and romantic, Mr. Snow. Be careful, you might get a bad rep for being a softy." He was so easy to tease and brought out my flirty side like no man ever had.

Gannon snorted. "Never really *slept* with anyone long enough to know, but I doubt I would have cuddled with any of them."

"I feel special then."

We fell into a comfortable silence, enjoying the quiet warmth of the dimly-lit room and the easy press of bodies in a cocoon of blankets.

"You are special, you know that, right?" Gannon asked, his voice very low and very close to my ear.

I wasn't ashamed of the whimper that escaped me. "Damn it, you can't say shit like that and expect me *not* to want to roll over and beg you to kiss me stupid."

Gannon chuckled, a deep, gravelly sound tinged with what I chose to believe was desire. "You've already got me acting stupid, so I guess it's only fair."

Rolling to face him, moaning when our hard cocks brushed together—and throwing up a prayer of thanksgiving for the decision to go commando as my bare legs grazed his flannel pants—I pressed my hands into his chest. "I very much want to take what you just said as consent, but my brain may be mush thanks to all the blood pooling in my dick. Have you changed your mind?"

"No."

My heart sank.

"I've wanted you from the moment I saw you. Just thought I could avoid the inevitable and be out of town before the temptation got too great." Gannon tipped my chin and brushed a scorching kiss over my lips. "I was wrong. Thought sleep would help clear my head and see things from a more rational, mature, level-headed side of things." He ran his hand down my back and cupped my ass. "I was wrong." Gannon smiled against my lips as his hand warmed my bare ass cheek. "Thought I could shut out the things you do to me, stay cool and detached until I made my escape." He rocked his hips into mine and we both groaned as our erections rubbed together. "I was wrong."

"What do you want?" I asked, my words a breathy whisper.

"Every part of you," Gannon answered before sealing our lips together and sweeping his tongue against mine, demanding and sure.

"Yes," I murmured into his mouth when we finally broke the kiss. At that moment, I would have handed him my heart, straight from my chest—I wanted absolutely everything with this man. This moment, a future, his love, a life together.

All.

Of.

It.

"I want that. Anything you want. I prepped. There should be lube in my bag, condoms too." I really wanted to tell him I'd been tested twice since my last sexual encounter over six months ago and I was on PrEP, but I'd always used condoms before and foregoing them this time would indicate Gannon was more than a hookup.

He is more than a hookup, dumbass. Don't you feel the way your damn heart is already gone for this man? It may seem too fast, but don't pretend you're not already head over heels.

"Slow." He teased fingers between my ass cheeks and pressed against my hole. "We've got time. This ass is mine, but we can wait."

I huffed out a frustrated sound.

"So impatient," he crooned at my ear. "I'll make you come, no worries."

"Please," I begged.

"Will you suck me?" Gannon asked and I thought they were the sexiest words I'd ever heard.

I nodded, my heart pounding in my chest, cock throbbing, mouth watering for my first taste of this gorgeous man.

Gannon shifted and brought me to a sitting position so he could yank the sleep-shirt over my head. Then he pushed me back down to lie on my side and knelt by my head, tapping his leaking cockhead against my lips.

I swiped my tongue over his slit, looking up at him to gauge his reaction. The way he cupped the back of my head and closed his eyes as if in silent prayer sent a surge of confident longing through me.

This man wanted me.

He may have been warring with himself over his place in the town or getting involved with me, but there was no doubt he wanted this—wanted me—as much as I wanted him.

Parting my lips, I sucked his cockhead into my mouth and swirled my tongue around the fleshy tip.

Gannon groaned and sifted fingers through my hair. "Fuck, Hayden. You look amazing on my cock, those pretty lips opening for me."

When I took him all the way to the back of my throat, he cursed and gripped the headboard. Falling into the perfect rhythm of stroking and sucking, I savored the saltiness of him on my tongue.

Gannon pulled away with a gasp and squeezed the base of his cock. "Too much," he bit out. "Don't wanna come yet."

Pouting slightly because I'd wanted to watch him shatter as I sucked him, I let him roll me to my back and settle himself between my spread legs.

Gannon kissed me, long and deep, as our cocks smeared precum between our stomachs. He moved from my lips to my jawline and down to my chest. Thumbing over my nipples and teasing them with his tongue, Gannon smiled when I writhed under him and gasped. "You like that? Noted," he whispered softly before sucking my nipple back between his lips.

He shifted to my side, his head at waist-level, he took my throbbing cock in his hand, and licked his lips like a man about to tuck into a feast when I moaned. "This okay?"

I nodded and gasped, "Yes."

Gannon licked my shaft before taking me deep into his hot mouth and I bucked on the bed. He chuckled around my dick and the vibrations had my balls drawing up tight. "You want my fingers?" he asked gruffly.

"Please," I begged. His touch, his kiss, the connection between us already so much more than anything I'd experienced before. Just like I'd known it would be.

Gannon slicked his first finger with spit and teased it around my hole. Gathering more moisture from his wet mouth, he returned to press into me, making me whimper at the brief sting of pleasure.

He worked his slick finger in and out as he bobbed his head on my cock, then popped off, leaving my cock throbbing and begging for more, dribbled spit onto two fingers, and slid them back into me.

The full stretch coupled with his warm, wet mouth taking my cock deep again had my balls aching and that familiar tingle starting at the base of my spine. I panted, "Gannon, please."

"You wanna come?" he taunted.

"Fuck, yes. Please."

He pressed his fingers deeper, brushing over my prostate and sending a jolt of pleasure through my body. I cried out as my release rocked me, hot spurts of cum splattering on my stomach and chest, Gannon watching me intently.

When my orgasm finally waned enough for Gannon to slip his fingers from my body, he pulled out, moved to his knees between my legs, and took his rock-hard cock in hand.

Watching him stroke himself as I floated on a cloud of blissed-out pleasure sent shockwaves of ecstasy through me.

The aloof, detached, skeptical man lost himself in the moment. Eyes on mine, he jerked himself hard and fast. With three more strokes, he grunted and groaned his release, long ropes of cum painting my stomach. Gannon moved so we were chest-to-chest, the slick cum mixing between us, our sensitive, spent cocks nestled together.

"That okay?" I asked, a bit hesitant that he'd freak out and try to bolt—although I wasn't sure where he'd go, maybe just deeper into his head instead of taking the moment of pleasure for what it was.

"Best ever," Gannon grumbled into my neck.

I couldn't help but giggle at the compliment. Yeah, he was probably still under the influence of an endorphin boost, but when a man like Gannon Snow says you were the best ever, you take it, even if it's likely not true.

Gannon eventually roused enough to grab a tissue and clean us up somewhat. "More sleep," he muttered as he pulled me close under the blankets. "Then breakfast."

Loving the snuggly, cuddly Gannon—even as my heart prepared to break when he left—I wiggled my ass against him. "And sex after breakfast? It's a snow day, can we just stay in bed all day?"

Gannon growled. "Sleep."

I woke a bit later to the smell of coffee, bacon, and eggs.

Surely, I was dreaming.

Pulling on a pair of socks with my extra-long flannel shirt, I brushed my teeth, washed my face, and made my way to the kitchen where I found Gannon plating up buttered toast, fried eggs, and bacon onto paper plates next to two steaming mugs.

Standing there, mouth agape, I tried to make sense of the scene in front of me. "Um…"

Gannon laughed. "You're not going to believe this." He handed me a plate and mug before ushering me to the table and tucking a blanket around my legs after I sat down. "Actually, you probably won't have any issue with it, it's just me still having a problem wrapping my head around it."

I cocked a brow and waited for Gannon to get his own plate and mug and join me at the table. Sipping from my drink, which turned out to be peppermint hot chocolate, I eyed him suspiciously over the plate of food—food which I *knew* we hadn't had the night before.

"So, I got up to pee and make coffee. On my way to the kitchen, I got curious about how much snow had fallen, so I opened the front door, right?"

I nodded, having no clue where the story was going.

"The door has a pile of snow, but it's not as deep as the yard since it's covered—looked like the snow was pretty heavy, not that kind that blows in the wind—anyway, right on top of the pile of snow in front of the door were five bags of groceries. No note, no footprints, nothing. Just butter, eggs, bacon, milk, bread, coffee, hot chocolate. Two containers that appear to be mashed potatoes with gravy and a thick stew of some sort. A rotisserie chicken, frozen lasagna, and breadsticks." Gannon's eyes bugged out as he spoke. "Who could have gotten up here? No footprints, no note. Nothing. No tire marks. How?"

I laughed and chomped on my toast as I waggled my brow.

Gannon groaned. "No. There's got to be a logical explanation."

"There is."

He eyed me over his coffee.

"Christmas magic," I sang.

He held his head in his hands. "I said *logical*, not some fantasy."

I shrugged. "If you come up with something better, let me know. I plan to enjoy the food and not worry about the how." Piling spoonfuls of fried egg onto my toast and topping it with bacon, I smirked around the mouthful as Gannon stewed.

The moment he finally just gave in and accepted he'd likely never know where the groceries had come from, his shoulders relaxed and he settled into his food.

We chatted over breakfast like we'd been a couple living in the hillside hideaway for years and years—my heart was definitely *way* too involved.

"Go on and shower or whatever you want to do," Gannon said, waving me out of the kitchen. "I'll clean this up."

Following him to the sink to put my empty mug in the soapy water, I snaked my arms around his waist and pressed a kiss to the back of his neck. "And what if I said what I wanted to do involved us spending all day in bed?"

Gannon tensed, groaning as I let my hand slowly trail down his abs to brush over his thick, hard cock. "We're supposed to be organizing today."

"I'm not even *supposed* to be here, but the universe had different plans. We'll be here tomorrow too—no way the snow will melt or get cleared until at least the day after, and that's only a possibility if the sun comes out and the temps soar." Stroking him through his flannel pants, I stood on my tiptoes to whisper, "I'll deal with the fallout when you leave, but I know I'll regret it if we don't take advantage of this time together."

Gannon was quiet for a moment, but he must have made a decision because he turned in my arms and backed me into the corner of the counter. With our bodies pressed together, his gray-blue eyes dark with desire, Gannon cupped the sides of my face and brought our lips together. What started as a chaste, sweet kiss quickly flamed to life as he owned my mouth, his hot, demanding tongue making me want to delve under his skin and stay there forever.

"Just for fun," he growled against my lips when we broke apart. "I'm leaving. I didn't come here looking for more. I'm not *made* for more. We have to keep feelings out of it."

"I can do that," I lied.

"Go start the shower, I'll be in as soon as I clean up in here." He sealed the promise with a kiss and swatted at my ass as I headed toward the bedroom.

Knowing we wouldn't have tons of hot water, I turned it on and climbed under the spray, doing a quick and thorough wash of all the important parts. Just as I rinsed off, the door slid open and a gloriously naked Gannon joined me.

I whimpered as he wrapped me in his arms and kissed me, bringing our solid erections together under the warm fall of water.

"If I suck you off in here, can you get off later too?" Gannon asked against my lips.

"Maybe," I panted into his mouth.

"Or maybe I just get you close in here and don't let you come until later," he suggested, making me moan in hot, needy anticipation.

He dropped to his knees and took my cock deep to the back of his throat as his hands parted my ass cheeks and a finger stroked over my hole. He continued teasing my pucker, but popped off my throbbing cock. "This tight little hole is mine," he said against the sensitive skin of my groin as he pressed his finger inside, making me cry out and lean against the tile for support. "You're gonna open up so pretty for me, stretch around my cock when you ride me."

His words had me weak in the knees and desperately thrusting the empty air looking for friction against my dick.

Gannon chuckled and added another finger, stretching me for later as he took my cock back between his lips. He sucked me deep before tonguing my slit and teasing up and down the sensitive underside.

"Gannon, please," I begged, my balls drawing tight and my dick begging for release. "Make me come." I knew he was just teasing me, not really trying to get me off.

"Not yet," he said. "You can wait a little longer, wanna watch you come with my cock stretching you open."

Whimpering, I clenched my ass around his probing fingers.

"Yeah, just like that," he growled. "Wanna feel this tight little ass grip my hard cock while you ride me."

I huffed out my frustration. "Then let's get out already," I whined.

Gannon chuckled as he slid his fingers from my ass and stood up. "You dry off and find the lube. Condoms?"

Biting my lip, I swallowed thickly. "I'm on PrEP and I've been tested twice since my last partner. Never went without before, so I'm good either way."

"Fuck," he grumbled. "Same here. *Never* gone without, but fuck if I don't want to with you."

"I'll put one out, we can decide when the time comes," I murmured against his lips, dipping my tongue in and savoring the flavor of my pre-cum on his tongue. "Hurry and wash up, don't keep me waiting."

Rushing through the drying-off process, I hurried to the bedroom and added another log to the fire so the room would stay toasty warm. Digging through my bag, I found the lube and condoms from my last trip to the city. I tossed one onto the bedside table and placed the lube beside it before crawling into the large bed.

The door from the bathroom opened and Gannon stalked toward me, his damp hair slightly mussed from a towel being run through it, his cock bobbing proudly, and his dark eyes honed in on me.

When he stopped next to the bed and reached out to stroke my cheek, I smiled nervously. "Why do I feel like I'm about to be eaten up by the big bad wolf?"

Gannon chuckled. "I'll give you a chance to play first, then that ass is mine." He joined me on the bed and I stretched out on top of him, loving the way our bodies fit so perfectly together.

"What do you like?" I asked, breathless with anticipation over having this man in my bed, free for the taking.

"With you? I'd probably agree to anything right about now," Gannon answered, his words gruff and full of desire.

"Fingers and tongue in your ass?" I asked, feeling bold and confident with Gannon in ways I'd never felt with other men.

A deep rumble escaped him and he pulled me close for a devouring kiss. Breathing deeply when we broke apart, he said, "Not something I do a lot of, but like I said, with you…"

"You'll tell me if you want me to stop?" I asked.

Gannon nodded. "Yeah."

I pressed kisses along his jaw and paused to suck and tease his nipples before licking his leaking cock like a lollipop. When Gannon's strong legs fell open for me, a surge of possessiveness filled my chest—I wanted this man to be mine. Sucking his balls into my mouth, teasing them with my tongue, I slowly made my way to tease his taint before flicking my tongue over his hole.

Loving the way he groaned, I gathered spit and smeared it around his entrance, spearing his pucker with my tongue. With one hand, I reached for his cock, stroking it slowly. With the other hand, I slicked my finger and pressed into Gannon's tight heat, whimpering as his muscles gripped me and he grunted his pleasure at my touch.

"Okay?" I asked, adding my tongue alongside my finger and working him into a frenzy.

Gannon cursed and panted out something resembling a yes. When I added a second finger, he groaned and pre-cum dribbled over my fist. "Fuck, Hayden, I can't take any more. I'm going to come if you keep that up."

As much as I was enjoying having my way with him, I wanted Gannon inside me when he unloaded. Slipping my fingers gently from his body, I swiped my tongue once more over his hole and moved to my hands and knees on the mattress.

"Fuck," Gannon mumbled, rolling to his knees to kneel between my spread legs. He grabbed pillows and shoved them under my hips, pressing my chest to the bed, and moving to his stomach so his mouth aligned perfectly with my ass. "Okay?" he asked.

Like a wanton little slut, I reached behind me and spread my ass cheeks for him, loving the growl escaping his chest before he licked me from taint to top and back again. His hot, wet tongue sent electrifying shivers through me, and I cried out as he speared me and teased me, opening me for him.

"Please, Gannon," I begged.

"Fuck, this ass," he mumbled against my hole. "Wanna make it mine."

"Do it, get inside me," I whimpered.

"I wanna watch you ride me," he said.

"Like this first." I wanted to feel him slide into me in the most primitive way.

Gannon grunted his agreement and reached for the lube, pausing for just a moment at the condom. When I heard the click of the lube lid but no crinkle of foil wrapping, I nearly swallowed my tongue. Taking a man bare was something neither of us had ever done and it felt like a huge thing. To share something like that after promising to keep feelings out of the equation was likely the stupidest thing I could do, but I didn't want to turn back.

With my hole lubed and his shaft slicked up, Gannon knelt between my legs and pressed the head of his cock against my entrance. As he slowly entered me, working his way in inch by inch, my body screaming at the invasion, Gannon rubbed a soothing hand on the small of my back. "Fuck, Hayden. So god damn good, look at you taking my dick. Opening for me so good," he murmured.

I sobbed as he bottomed out, his balls pressing against me as his big hands gripped my hips. With slow, easy thrusts, Gannon worked me open and eased the stinging pain.

"You good?" he asked as he increased the speed of his thrusts.

"Fuck, yeah," I moaned. "Wanna ride you, but fuck it's so good."

"Prettiest hole I've ever seen stretched around my cock," he whispered as he stretched out over me, bringing his chest to my back, propping himself on his elbows, and thrusting into me as he pressed my hips into the pillows.

When the head of his cock brushed my prostate, I knew we needed to switch positions if I didn't want things to be over way too soon.

"Roll over," I said.

"Fuck, yes," Gannon said, pulling from me slowly and rolling to his back.

I pushed the pillows away and straddled his waist, reaching behind me to guide his hot, dripping cock back to my greedy hole.

Lowering myself onto him, loving the grip of his hands on my hips, I took him deep. When my ass pressed against him, his hot, silky flesh buried to the hilt, I leaned forward and thumbed his nipples. His sharp gasp and quick thrust of his hips had me whimpering. The tight stroke of his hand around my dick made my ass clench and we both cried out.

"Ride me," he demanded. "Work those sexy hips, show me what that pretty little ass can do."

Wanting nothing more than to lose myself with this man, to feel his hot cum shoot inside me as I painted myself on his chest, I leaned forward to grip the headboard and began rocking my hips in a front-back grinding motion, each movement bringing a zap of contact between that sweet bundle of nerves and the plump head of Gannon's cock.

"Fuck, Hayden," Gannon growled. "Look at you on my dick. So damn good."

We lost ourselves in the rhythm of our bodies. The scent of wood smoke and sex filled the room, the air alive with the crackling of the fire and the slapping of sweaty skin as we savored our connection and chased our release.

"Can I come inside you?" Gannon asked.

My breath caught on a gasp. "Fuck, yeah. Please."

"Then I want you to fuck my face and come down my throat," he added, his words making my balls draw up tight.

I shifted slightly so Gannon could plant his feet and thrust up into me hard and fast. His pistoning hips rocked me, his cock slamming into me was just this side of painful as he owned my ass. Soon though, Gannon's thrusting hips froze on the upstroke and he grunted, his throbbing cock exploding in my ass.

He rode out his release buried inside me before gripping my hips and urging me forward. "Let me suck you," he said as his spent cock slipped from my ass.

I moved up his chest and whimpered when he took my ready-to-detonate cock between his lips and swallowed me down. "Fuck, Gannon, not going to last."

His eyes met mine, his lips stretched around my cock, his dark hair streaked with silver a perfect contrast with my pale skin and russet-colored hair. He said nothing, just gripped my hips and pressed me to fuck his mouth. When he slid two fingers between my ass cheeks and pushed his leaking load back into my tight hole, I lost any semblance of control and shot down the back of his throat with a cry of pleasure. Gannon's moan around my shaft drove out the final pulse of cum before I collapsed on his chest, our spent cocks nestled together as we savored the exquisite high of what we'd just shared.

Several moments later—hell, I may have fallen asleep—he cupped my ass and murmured in my ear. "You okay?"

"So damn okay. If all we've got is this week, we need to do that as many times as possible." I kept my voice light and teasing, but I meant every word I said. To hell with heartbreak, I couldn't pass up the chance to give myself to Gannon over and over until he left.

"Anyone ever tell you you're trouble?" Gannon groused against my ear, but I heard the smile in his words and felt the evidence of his arousal valiantly attempting to re-energize against my belly.

"No one's ever really taken the time to know me that well," I answered, suddenly feeling vulnerable.

Gannon's warm arms tightened around me. "Damn fools," he murmured. "Probably setting us both up for a major crash and burn, but I don't know how to stay away from this. It's too good."

"Is that just the sex talking?" I asked, hoping for one answer and fearing another.

"Don't I wish? Would make things a lot easier." Gannon pressed a kiss to my neck. "We know this is temporary, no matter what else gets involved. As long as we keep that in mind, we can have some fun before it has to end."

I got the feeling Gannon's words were as much for himself as they were for me.

Problem was, I already knew I was in big trouble—more specifically, my heart was at risk for sure.

CHAPTER 9

Gannon

MY THOUGHTS WERE RACING, chugging along as loudly as the damn train blowing through town and keeping me awake despite having a sleepy, snuggly Hayden tucked against me.

I was in so much damn trouble.

If it weren't for the weather, and if I knew what was good for me, I'd march myself down to my ridiculous rental and drive straight out of town without looking back.

The moment the roads were clear enough, I'd do just that.

Because I *did* know what was good for me.

And it wasn't falling head-over-heels for a beautiful small-town guy.

It wasn't letting feelings take over and trap me in the middle of nowhere.

Why not? Sure, the place is small, but have you ever felt so content? And Hayden may be the poster boy for a local, but have you ever been this fucked up over a guy?

I pushed the thoughts away. I didn't want to think about the town or Hayden. Didn't want to think about what it meant that I was so comfortable in my grandfather's house.

Didn't want to examine the crazy-fast, ridiculous feelings swirling in my gut over Hayden.

No. Not now. Not ever.

I'd finish up at the house and head home.

Home.

LA.

My apartment.

A chill washed over me when I thought of my lonely existence on the west coast.

Working twelve and fifteen hours a day to stay busy and avoid people.

Dinners alone in front of spreadsheets unless some young twink had teased my dick enough to earn his way into my bed.

Occasional dates if certain men were non-annoying enough to keep around for a spell.

I tried to imagine Hayden in LA.

He'd love it and hate it all at the same time.

And I'd love showing it to him, yet I'd hate dirtying him with the big city—hate dulling his sparkle.

As the damn train whistle sounded shrilly, I focused on the man in my arms. We had a few more days. I'd be back in LA for the holiday and Hayden could throw himself into teaching, the store, and his Christmas pageant work. He'd be so busy he'd likely forget about me before my plane even touched down.

And you? You think you're going to forget him? He's burned into your skin, the taste of him scaled on your tongue. Will you ever see fucking eggnog and not think of him? Bowties? Suspenders? Crazy socks?

Pain clenched in my chest at the thought of not having Hayden in my arms.

Not having him in my life.

So, just stay put. See how it goes.

No.

Everyone would be better off if we kept feelings out of it and went our separate ways like we'd planned from the beginning.

I didn't know how to deal with what my heart begged to feel for Hayden.

I didn't know how to do a real relationship.

And I definitely didn't know how to become a small-town resident.

So, even though you're in love with the man, you're going to walk away from what might be the best thing that's ever happened to you?

My huff of annoyance made Hayden snuffle in his sleep and burrow closer to me.

Not in *love*.

I didn't even know what love was.

I most definitely didn't know how to be *in* it.

Bullshit. You loved Joseph. You loved this town. If you'd be honest with yourself, you still love it. And you've fallen hard for Hayden.

Nope.

I wasn't going there.

A couple more days of sex.

Sex *only*.

And then I'd leave.

And everyone would be better off.

Period.

End of story.

Somehow, even with another train roaring through a bit later, I finally managed to fall asleep.

With the most gorgeous, amazing man I'd ever had the pleasure of knowing cuddled in my arms.

I was so fucked. I *had* to get out of town and away from Hayden. Get my head back on straight.

I wasn't sure how much longer I could fight the pull of the damn town.

Not sure how much more my heart could stand—it wanted Hayden in the worst way, but it wasn't fair to subject the man to someone who didn't know how to love him the way he deserved.

I woke sometime later to Hayden's ass pressed against my cock. Not only was my dick immediately on board with whatever he wanted to do, my heart flip-flopped at the thought of waking up with Hayden every damn day for the rest of our lives.

Ignoring the foolish organ, I concentrated on the warm press of Hayden's ass against me.

"Something you want?" I asked, voice gruff with sleep and desire.

"Want you to fuck me," Hayden pleaded. "Please."

I slid a finger between his ass cheeks and found him slick with lube and cum. Groaning, I pressed the head of my cock to his messy hole and pushed into him. The sighs and heat between us sounded like coming home and I buried my face in his neck as I pumped into him.

No feelings.

Only sex.

The best sex of my life.

With a man I didn't want to let out of my sight.

But still just sex.

I did not love this man.

Hayden threw his head back with a whimper as I thrust hard and deep. "Fuck, Gannon, fuck. So good. Fuck."

With one arm wrapped around Hayden's chest and the other hand splayed on his soft, smooth abs, I pumped into him with everything I had. "Do you wanna come like this or in my mouth?" I murmured at his ear.

Hayden sobbed. "Like this. Please, Gannon. Touch me."

My hand immediately went to his hard, leaking cock and

stroked him in the same rhythm as my dick slamming into him.

When Hayden cried out, his dick spurting over my fist and his ass clenching around me, I thrust into him once, twice, three more times before unloading with a groan. As the image of my cum painting the walls of his tight channel filled my head, I buried my face at his shoulder and rode out my orgasm as he writhed against me.

"I swear I've never had sex this good," Hayden panted with a blissed-out smile as he turned his head for a kiss. "I'm sure you're used to it, but oh my god, I never knew it could be this good."

Maybe it was the sex fogging my brain, maybe it was the haze of the fucking little Christmas town, maybe it was the connection simmering between us like a pot of hot apple cider, but I opened my damn mouth and said, "Best I've ever had."

Hayden winced as he pulled himself from my spent dick and turned to face me. "For real? All those guys you've slept with and this is the best?"

I could have lied. Could have shut it all down and kept to my promise of no feelings, just sex.

Instead, I cupped his face and made love to his mouth before pulling away and nodding. "No one else has ever compared to this."

My chest tightened when those pretty navy-blue eyes sparkled and got suspiciously bright. I never wanted to let this man go. Wanted to spend the rest of my life holding him, sharing fiery hot pleasure with him, calling him mine.

Never in my life had I wanted to get to know a man the way I wanted to get to know Hayden. Never had I wanted to share parts of myself with a guy.

Until Hayden.

My pretty little small-town boy.

We ended up showering again and putting together a hodge-podge of food for lunch before crawling back in bed with a battery pack, Hayden's laptop, and a few movies.

The office could wait.

The next day would come soon enough.

For someone who doesn't want feelings to get involved, you're sure being awfully sentimental about making the most of the time you have with Hayden.

I ignored the little voice in my head.

A guy could be interested in getting as much great sex as possible without becoming all heart-fluttery.

What? He could.

I could.

After our third movie, Hayden's laptop chimed and he hit accept.

"Candy, hi. Everything okay?" he asked as the image of an older woman filled the screen. Another woman joined her. "Ginger, hi."

"We talked to your dad and he said he'd heard from you, but we wanted to be sure you were doing okay up there on the hill," Candy said.

Ginger waggled her brow. "Looks like our concerns were all for naught, I'd say you're doing just fine."

In a split second, I realized Hayden and I were shoulder to shoulder, propped against the headboard in bed. The only reason we had clothes on was because we'd dressed to ward off the chill after our showers. Otherwise, had they caught us earlier, we would have been shirtless.

Hell, we would have been completely naked.

Hayden chuckled. "Well, there's very little furniture in the house and no heat beyond our little electric heaters and the fireplace, so we're keeping to one room at a time. Today's a snow day with movies. How are things in town?"

It amazed me how quickly Hayden breezed right through a very convincing explanation without so much as blushing. He knew damn well we'd been doing all sorts of deliciously dirty things in that bed just hours before—and we'd be right back at it shortly if I had my way—yet, he easily brushed off the older women's suggestive comments without blinking.

"Things are just fine down here. Smith and Johnson started plowing some streets earlier. Figure Carter will do the same once he gets his truck dug out. Your dad's already got their driveway and street cleared thanks to his tractor," Candy said. "We'll likely be back to business tomorrow— albeit trudging through snow—so I'd say you boys should be cleared by late tomorrow afternoon or early morning by the next."

As badly as I wanted to escape—I really didn't like to be forced to stay somewhere—a tiny part of me ached at the knowledge I'd be able to leave soon.

Yeah, it was for the best, but it was going to hurt like a bitch no matter how much I'd told myself to keep feelings out of it.

"Well, while we've got you," Ginger said with a wink. "Gannon, how are you doing, hon?"

"Oh, um, I'm good, ma'am. Thank you."

"Joseph didn't want to leave too much work for you," Ginger said.

"But he wanted there to be enough to keep you in town for a while. He was sneaky that way." Candy smiled and took Ginger's hand. "I'm not sure how much you knew about your grandfather, but we loved him very much."

Oh, god.

I didn't want details of my grandfather's sex life.

"Now, don't traumatize the boy," Ginger scolded softly.

"I'm not going to draw diagrams," Candy joked. "The three of us fell in love over many years and the last couple decades we had with him were an absolute blessing. So much love and friendship. That man was the most caring, generous, and funny person we ever had the pleasure of knowing—and I'm not just saying that because he's dead. He was truly one-of-a-kind."

"He was," I said, my heart pounding and emotions twisting in my gut.

"Did you know he tried to leave Saint Nicholas Crossing once?" Ginger asked.

My eyes jerked to the screen. "What? No. When? I thought he loved this place."

"Oh, he did," Ginger said. "But the three of us got a wild hair we'd move to the city and do big things. Now, this was back when we were still flirting with the idea of loving each other. We figured we'd move to the city, continue doing what we loved, and be happy as could be."

"What happened?" Hayden asked.

"We were there for about a year and Joseph was miserable," Candy said. "We weren't much better. When he finally couldn't stand it any longer, he broke down and told us he wanted to go back. By that time, we'd fallen into bed and our years of friendship had sparked into a lot more—but he was worried about the Crossing not being enough for us. Thought we'd get bored."

"But you all came back?" Hayden asked.

"We did. When a place and its people are in your heart, you'll always feel the pull," Ginger said. "We could have made it work—the three of us—in the city, but Joseph would have been unhappy and we could do what we wanted from anywhere. We headed back here and never looked back. He increased his efforts ten-fold at The Heart and we poured ourselves into our small-businesses."

"Did you?" The words spilling from my mouth unbidden.

The women each cocked a brow.

"Get bored. Wish you were somewhere else?" I asked.

They smiled.

"Not even once," Candy said.

"We can travel if needed—although, we really don't do much of that," Ginger said. "We have everything we need here. Technology is a wonderful thing. We keep busy. Losing Joseph has been hard, but coming back here was the right thing for us."

Candy leaned over and kissed Ginger's cheek. "Once the three of us admitted our hearts were with each other *and* this crazy little town, there was nothing we couldn't do."

"No use fighting what the heart wants," Ginger said with a soft smile.

"Well, we've kept you boys long enough with our walk down memory lane. Give us a call if you need anything. Otherwise, we'll see you once the hill road is clear enough to get back to town."

Hayden closed the laptop.

We sat quietly for a moment.

"Well, that was interesting," Hayden said. "I didn't realize the three of them had been together so long. It's sad he's gone, but I'm glad they have each other."

I grunted, reaching for the laptop and putting it on the bedside table.

I didn't want to think about my grandfather leaving town and being drawn back in. Didn't want to think about this damn little town having its claws so deep in him he couldn't even make it in the city. And I most definitely didn't want to think about what my heart wanted.

It didn't matter.

What it *wanted* wasn't what it needed—not what Hayden needed either.

I wasn't going to bring my fucked up past and inability to form a loving relationship into his life and screw him up.

My parents ruined me.

I wouldn't do that to Hayden.

You maybe haven't ever been in *love, but Joseph taught you how to love. You're rusty, but even you can admit that what you feel for Hayden is the easiest, most fulfilling thing you've ever done. Don't ignore what the two of you might have.*

Ignoring the thoughts, I stripped Hayden's shirt over his head and rolled him to his back. "Any chance you've got one of those bowties and your suspenders?"

He giggled as I pinned his hands over his head and buried my face in his armpit. "No, why?"

"Almost bust a nut every time I think of you riding me in a jock with a bowtie and suspenders," I growled.

"How about we make up for my lack of accessories by taking advantage of the fire and that sturdy chair?" Hayden bit his lip.

I glanced over my shoulder at the chair in question in front of the toasty fire. "Not going to replace my bowtie and suspenders fantasy, but it'll do. You're not too sore?"

"I'm good as long as you don't go full-force this time around."

We rolled from bed and I threw another log on the fire before stripping naked.

Taking my place on the chair, I let Hayden choose whether he wanted to face me or the fire. After handing me the lube, he straddled me, his pretty ass hovering over my rock-hard cock.

Once I'd slicked his hole and my cock, I pressed myself against his pretty little pucker and held onto his hips as he lowered himself onto my shaft with breathy little whimpers escaping him as he took me deep.

I was leaving.

I had to.

But for the rest of my life, I'd remember Hayden's tight heat, his firm hips under my hands, and the glorious sight of my cock sliding in and out of his ass as he rode me.

I held him tight and let him come apart in my arms as I poured myself into him.

Later that night, after dinner and another round of sex—this time just mouths and fingers because I knew he had to be sore—Hayden lay cuddled against me as I read more of *Holly Hills Christmas*.

"You like it?" he asked.

"As much as I don't want to like it, I do."

"Why don't you want to like it?" Hayden asked, trailing his fingers over my chest, teasing my nipples and making my cock wonder if it could go another round.

"It's not real life. It's a nice little fantasy, but real people don't get love like this," I said, my heart aching with how badly I wanted what Vince and Kota had found.

"Maybe not often—and maybe not exactly like in fictional stories—but I think true love and blissful happiness is out there for most of us," Hayden said, pressing a kiss against the corner of my lips. "We just have to be open to it happening."

Grunting a non-committal sound, I finished the last few sentences of the chapter and put the book aside.

I needed to focus on finishing the house and getting back to LA.

But for the rest of the night, I'd give in and let myself savor each and every moment I had left with Hayden.

The next morning, I took one last moment to luxuriate in Hayden's body. Slow, easy, perfect. Then we showered and spent the day orbiting around each other as we organized, talked about the most random things, did a bit of our own work, and basically just co-existed peacefully with the air between us only slightly tinged with sadness, tension, and...annoyance?

Hayden seemed slightly annoyed with me—and really, I couldn't blame him, I was annoyed with myself.

This questioning, unsure version of me wasn't what I was used to.

But I'd also never been punched in the face with an avalanche of emotions—loss, guilt, desire, need...*love*.

When Ellen texted that she was going to call me, I piled into my winter gear and told Hayden I was going to get some fresh air.

He cocked a brow my way.

"What? It's cold, but not *that* cold, right?" I shrugged and wrapped the scarf around my neck.

Thumbing Ellen's number as I slipped my earbuds into my ears, I shoved the phone into my pocket and waited for my right-hand to answer the call.

"I thought I was calling you," she said in way of greeting.

"Sorry, I needed to put gloves on and they're bulky when trying to tap the screen. What's up?"

"Why are you wearing gloves?"

I chuckled. "It's damn cold here right now. They're a necessity."

"Did Hayden kick you out?"

"What? No, why?"

"You're voluntarily outside in the cold?"

I shrugged under the heavy jacket. "It's not *that* bad. You kinda get used to it." I glanced around the snowy landscape, my breaths coming in puffs. "It's actually kinda pretty when you take the time to enjoy it."

"Who are you and what have you done with Gannon Snow?"

"I'm still here, just saying it's not as bad as I feared. I'll be back soon."

"What? Why? You miss LA that badly?"

I stared at the brightly sparkling landscape. Did I miss LA? Not in the slightest. "It's not that I miss LA, but it's best if I get back. Probably heading to the airport later today." My words felt hollow.

"Oh, um, that's what…that's what I was calling about. You can't come back."

"What? Why?"

"Mold."

"Mold?"

"Yeah, they're, um, spraying for mold in your building. And maybe some bugs, I think. I went to get your mail and saw signs."

"My apartment has mold and bugs?"

Ellen cleared her throat. "Not *your* apartment, but a couple around you. I think. No need to come back yet—it would just be a hassle. I'll tell you when it's clear."

I sighed and pinched the bridge of my nose.

"You said it's not that bad there, right?" Ellen asked.

"It's not that bad, but I need to be gone."

"Why?"

I had no words as I stared out across the snow-covered hill.

"Why, Gannon?"

"I just do," I answered softly.

"Does your need to flee have anything to do with a sweet, cute, sexy little small-town boy who's captured your heart?"

"My heart has no business being in love."

Ellen smile could be heard across the phone line. "I didn't say anything about love."

Clearing my throat, I gritted out, "Yeah, well, maybe I did."

"Why would you run from that?"

"I don't know how to love. You know what my parents were like."

"I also know what your grandfather was like from your many stories. And I know *you*. You've been blessed with a job you can do from anywhere, a fairly bomb-ass assistant—if I do say so myself—why would you try to get away from the only man who's ever jumped right in with both feet and broken through that frozen heart of yours?" Ellen asked.

"I don't want to fuck things up."

"You've turned everything you've ever set your mind to into a huge success, why would this be any different?"

"Business shit, real estate, money…not relationship stuff. I've never had a real relationship and I don't want to hurt Hayden if it turns out I can't do it."

Ellen tsked. "Gannon, you're one of my dearest friends, but you need to pull your head from your ass. I think this is a situation where you, one, just need to let go and take a chance. And two, you and Hayden may work out precisely because you've never had a relationship. You know exactly how you felt with all those other men—that's why things with Hayden are so different."

"What if I end up hating it here?" I asked. "Hayden loves it, I couldn't ask him to leave."

"Hayden also loves you—maybe I'm assuming things, but just go with it—he'd likely be willing to do what it takes."

"No, I wouldn't ask him to leave."

"You're so certain you'd get bored and hate it?"

I huffed in frustration. "Haven't been bored yet, but I've also known I'm leaving."

"Outside of your business-related work, can you see things in the town you'd want to work on?"

Immediately, thoughts of the store came to mind. "There's the store—it's great, but it could be even better. This old house could use some updates—I haven't done any kind of handyman type work since Joseph taught me. But I'm good with my hands and the right YouTube video. If I fuck it up, I have the money to pay someone to do it." Visions of town council and school board floated through my mind. Joseph had been on those at one time or another. Would it be pathetic for me to think I could do the same? "I just don't want people thinking I'm trying to take his place," I said, voicing one of my many concerns.

"From what I've heard, no one could take your grandpa's place. But that doesn't mean you can't bring your own brand of greatness to the town. Give it some time." Ellen clucked her tongue. "Now, I have to go."

"You'll tell me when the mold is gone?"

"What?"

I raised a brow. "The mold that's keeping me from my apartment?"

"Oh, right. Yes, of course."

I pulled a glove off and ended the weird call.

Shoving my fingers back into the toasty-warm glove, I glanced up at the bright blue sky, the sun shining fiercely as it tried to melt the snow.

"Holiday magic, huh?" I asked the air around me.

Stretching my arms out wide, I turned in a circle, the cold enveloping me as my heart beat rapidly.

"Show me, then. If this *magic* is so real, make me believe. Give me a sign that my place is here."

The front door opened and Hayden gave me a strange look. "You're needed in here."

I pursed my lips and gave the sky a look. "Cute, but that wasn't what I meant."

Heading inside, with the sound of a distant train growing

louder, I found Hayden in the kitchen with big bowls of soup and buttered bread.

"Ellen okay?" he asked as we sat down at the table.

"Yeah, she's good."

We ate silently for a while until I took a final bite of soup and pushed back from the table.

"If I asked you to, would you ask me to stay?" The question flowed from my lips with absolutely no permission, but I couldn't take it back.

Hayden smiled gently and put down his spoon. "If I thought it was the right thing to do, I would ask you to stay in a heartbeat."

My heart plummeted. "But you don't think it's the right thing?"

He leaned forward, elbow on the table, chin in hand. "Do I think *this* is the right thing?" He gestured between us. "Without a doubt, one hundred percent. Never felt anything more right."

"But you don't want me to stay?"

"Don't put words in my mouth," he said. "I can't ask you to stay because staying has to be something you feel in your gut. Staying has to be something your heart tells you to do. You have to feel that Saint Nicholas Crossing—with or without me—is the place you belong. It can't be because I want you to stay more than my next breath."

"All I've ever wanted in life—outside of shutting myself away from any kind of connections—is to be wanted and loved. And now I've got this huge decision to make and you won't help?" I stood and walked my dishes to the sink.

Hayden joined me by the sink. "I get that you're stressed right now, but stop with the childish shit. You should know I want you here more than anything I've ever wanted in my life. But it's not my place to ask you to stay. I won't be the reason you stay and end up hating it."

"What if I *do* stay and end up hating it?"

Hayden shrugged. "We talk about it and work it out. If you stay—and choose to be in a relationship with me—we'll be in it together." He placed a hand on my shoulder. "But *you* have to fight your demons and decide if you want to be here. You're wanted—by more than just me—and welcome to be here. No one expects you to be your grandpa. But there's only one person who can make the decision to stay or leave. Stay and open your heart, learn to let people in, learn to feel, hopefully with me by your side if you'll have me. Or leave. Go back to the way things were before. I'd guess it would be easier in some ways. Stay closed off, detached, focus just on the money and success. Probably wouldn't be a *bad* life, but it's definitely not what you'd get here." He leaned in and kissed my cheek. "And *you* have to decide which of those you want."

A horn honked outside and pulled us from whatever little bubble we were in. Hayden rushed to the window and then threw open the door with a wave.

"It's Smith and Johnson, they've got the road cleared."

I swallowed thickly.

Maybe *that* was my sign?

"Wow, that was quick," I said.

"Probably wouldn't happen so quick in the city," Hayden said. "Although, probably would have had more warning of a big snow heading our way in the city too. But it was a heavy, wet snow—no real drifts to get through. The sun coming out and temperatures getting above freezing helped a lot. Plus, our folks with plows can focus just on our roads and not have to worry about city departments making demands."

"Yeah, lucky us," I said. All I'd wanted was to be able to leave, but now that I could, I wanted to hide away in the house with Hayden forever.

We were quiet as we finalized things around the house.

We packed everything up, unplugged the heaters, shut down the electric water heater, and loaded the truck.

Refusing to look at the house I'd loved so much growing up—the house where Hayden and I had shared so many quiet, intimate moments…where'd I'd admitted to myself I was in love with this beautiful man in spite of knowing him for almost no time—I kept my eyes straight ahead as Hayden pointed the truck down the driveway toward the steep road.

"You want to come to my place?" Hayden asked quietly once we'd reached the base of the hill road.

Clearing my throat, unsure of *everything*, I shook my head. "Probably need to head to my car."

Hayden's jaw clenched, but he nodded. "Yeah, okay."

When we reached the parking lot next to the park, I cursed aloud. "What the fuck? Where's my car?"

I pulled up the email app on my phone and cursed again. A confirmation from earlier in the day that the car had been picked up by the company at the request of my assistant and there was nothing else I needed to do.

Pinching the bridge of my nose, I took a deep breath.

You wanted a sign.

I wanted a sign, not Ellen meddling.

"Can you take me to the motel? I'll get a room until I can get a ride out of here."

Hayden huffed. "You have to be one of the most stubborn, emotionally-stunted people I've ever met. But yeah, I'll take you to the damn motel."

Before I could throw open my door and escape, Hayden gripped my hand.

"I need you to hear this. I love you. I think it started years ago, but it became real at the house. I know it's too quick. I know it's crazy. But I love you. I do want you to stay, but I respect that it's a decision you have to make on your own." Hayden leaned over and brushed a kiss over my lips. "There's something here and you can't deny it, I know you can't. But your head and heart have to be on board. If you think you can live with the cold, the perpetual Christmas, the busybodies, and the holiday magic, you know where to find me."

Then I found myself paying for a tiny yet clean and cozy little room, flopping down on the bed, and wallowing in self-pity and uncertainty as Hayden's words echoed through my head.

When the damn shrill train whistle busted into my thoughts and the rumble shook me to the bone, I reached for Tylenol in my bag. I'd take some medicine and try to sleep. Then I'd call for a ride to the airport the next day.

Hayden was right. Going back to the way things were would be the easiest.

The old Gannon knew what to expect from his life.

No attachments.

No feelings.

Same old, same old.

No opening myself up.

No learning how to love.

My fingers brushed over a sharp corner as I rummaged for the headache pills.

Pulling out the envelope with my name on it, I stared at it for a full minute.

The card from Joseph.

Scared to death of what it might say, yet unable to stop myself, I ripped into it and opened the card, unfolding the letter that fell out.

Dear Gannon,

If you're reading this, it means I'm gone. More than anything, I hope you know just how much I love you and how very proud I am of you. We maybe never got to live out my dream of you here in St.

Nicholas Crossing, but I'm hoping since you're reading this, maybe you'll be able to fulfill part of my wish.

Let me start by saying that I loved your father. I wish every day that things had been different between my son and me, but that's something that's taken many years to work through. How he ended up so jaded, so lost, so full of hatefulness when he came from two people who weren't that way at all, I'll never know. I do wish you'd been able to know your grandmother, she was such a special person and she would have loved you so much.

Your father was such a lost soul. Maybe it was because he never knew his mother. Maybe it was just the way he was wired. Maybe I did something wrong in raising him. I likely won't ever know.

I want to say he loved you—parents love their children—but he was so full of hatefulness, so focused on negativity, I'm not sure he was capable of loving anyone other than himself.

His last words to me before he passed on were, "Leave Gannon out of your ridiculous small-town dreams. He's more like me than he realizes. He'll eventually realize what a quack you are and never look back. You may have hopes for the Snow name to continue in that Podunk little town, but it ended when I left and I'll be damned if Gannon ever takes his place beside you. He is so much more than The Crossing. Full of so much potential to carry on the Snow name in my footsteps, not yours."

Your father wrote those words in a birthday letter to me a few years before he died. I don't share his message with you to manipulate, but I wanted you to know what his expectations for you were.

Perhaps you wish to follow in his footsteps.

Perhaps his words will mean something to you.

I leave them for you so that you can make your own decisions.

I never gave up on having you settle in St. Nicholas Crossing with me, I'm just sorry I wasn't able to hang on long enough to see it happen.

You are not your father.

You are worth more than what your parents taught you.

If you choose to stay in town, please know this place is rich in love and friendship—and don't overlook the magic, I know you're skeptical, but have an open mind—and these people will welcome you with open arms. Not only because you're my flesh and blood, but because they recognize good when they see it.

And that's what you are, Gannon.

I hate that your parents ever made you doubt it.

I hate that I wasn't able to reach you.

I hate that you've shut yourself off.

But I know what this place can do for people.

I know you can find love and acceptance and happiness here, if you'll just give it a chance.

If you're looking for a sign, this is it.

Be happy, be loved.

Love,

    Grandpa Joseph

My eyes blurred as I took in the little drawing at the bottom of the letter. Railroad tracks, trees, a train, and a sign with the words St. Nicholas Crossing- Where Your Heart Finds What It's Looking For.

Damn him.

Damn Joseph for knowing.

Damn this town for digging its claws into me.

I chuckled, tears escaping the corner of my eyes.

Damn me for fighting it for so long.

And damn my heart for soaring at the thought of making my home here.

Could I really do it? Was it truly that easy?

Take a risk. Don't let your dad win. The least you can do is give it a shot. For Joseph.

For Joseph.

Yeah, for Joseph.

But for more than just my grandpa.

This town and its people deserved a shot.

Hayden and I deserved a shot.

If he'd have me.

CHAPTER 10

Hayden

After I dropped the most bull-headed man I'd ever met at The Crossing Motel, I did what I did best.

I threw myself into work and focusing on others.

I refused to listen to any of the whispered words referring to Gannon still being in town. As much as I wanted him to stay, I couldn't put my life on hold for him. If he decided to stick around, I'd be there—if he wanted me to be there.

If he decided to leave, I'd eventually have to nurse my broken heart, but for the time being, I'd hide away from the hurt.

Outside of telling him how I felt, the ball was in Gannon's court.

A couple days before Christmas, my students were beyond *done* with learning—and I couldn't blame them—so I let my last period class come to the auditorium and help with the final rehearsal for the Christmas pageant. It was a good distraction for them and for me as we put finishing touches on costumes, set design, and music.

By the time showtime rolled around that evening, I was a bundle of nerves, but I knew the kids would be great. The pageant was always a fun way to kick off our winter break from school and get the whole town into the holiday spirit— not that they really needed any help.

"Too bad Gannon wasn't able to be here," Mom said as she helped one of the reindeer straighten their antlers.

"Mom," I started warningly.

I'd shared just a bit about Gannon and his choice to leave.

My parents had insisted Gannon wouldn't leave—or, if he did, he'd be back.

As much as I wanted to believe them, I wouldn't allow myself to.

I was angry with Gannon.

But I also understood his fears.

It was frustrating to watch him struggle, but I knew he had to deal with things on his own. First, because he needed to prove to himself he could open up and make a change for the better *on his own*—me being in the middle of that would maybe make it easier, but in the long run, Gannon needed to know he did it himself.

Second, if we stood any chance of building something real between us, we both needed to know Gannon had chosen to stay for the right reasons and not just because we'd started up a whirlwind romance.

These were facts and I knew them to be true all the way to the toes of my crazy socks, but that didn't make it any easier to wait for Gannon to make his decision.

We hadn't been apart that long, but I missed him so much it physically hurt.

And my head had already convinced itself Gannon was gone for good.

But just when I'd tell myself I needed to shake it off and just bury myself in work, my heart would send up a last-ditch effort to convince me to give it a little more time.

Moving here would be a complete upheaval of his life. Give him time. It's a huge decision. But you two had something real, he wouldn't give up on it without a fight.

I wanted more than anything to believe that.

But Gannon had been pretty closed-off when I left him at the motel.

Guarding his heart was how he'd made it through most of his adult life. It was what he did, what he knew. What made me think he'd opt to do anything differently this time around just because I'd gone and fallen in love with him?

You don't want him to change for you my heart reminded me. *You want him to change because it's what's right for him.*

I sighed as I glanced out at the audience from backstage.

Yeah, I wanted Gannon to do what was right for him.

But if it turned out he decided to settle in St. Nicholas Crossing and continue what we'd started, I sure as shit wasn't going to be upset about it.

The pageant started and I lost myself in the production.

The songs—a perfect mix of traditional and modern holiday music—sounded amazing and the snippets of lines the children shared were absolutely adorable.

By the time the show ended, I couldn't help the huge smile on my face. Hugs and compliments ensued. It was times like these that made me truly appreciate the special place I called home.

"You were really in your element tonight. Great show."

I whipped my head around and barely contained the gasp of delight when I saw Gannon standing there with a sheepish smile. I was in his arms within seconds, not giving a shit that the whole town was watching.

"Thank you," I whispered. "I didn't know you were going to be here."

Well, duh.

I hadn't even known for sure he was still in town, let alone he'd come to the pageant.

"Wasn't sure either. You have plans after this?" Gannon asked, his words low and gruff at my ear.

I shook my head. "No, just cleaning up and heading home."

"Can I meet you there?"

Nodding dumbly, I finally released him. "Yeah, um, give me an hour?"

"See you there."

After the quickest clean-up of all clean-ups—and huge thanks to my parents for finishing up for me so I could rush home—I all but sprinted up my steps and launched myself into a fast and thorough shower to wash off the hay, paint, sawdust, and sweat from the day.

When I emerged from the bathroom, I yelped to find Gannon at the kitchen counter.

"You didn't lock your door," he said.

"Not something we do a lot of around here."

"Guess I'll have to get used to that."

My heart soared.

"You're staying?"

Gannon handed me a glass of eggnog with a wink and ushered me toward the couch.

"I loved seeing you so happy tonight. You've got such talent, you're so good at what you do—directing, teaching, the store, everything," Gannon said.

Swallowing thickly around the smooth, creamy eggnog, I croaked out, "Thank you. That means a lot."

"All I wanted to do when I came here was show up, take care of business, and leave. In and out. No distractions. No attachments. It's how I've lived my life and run my business for decades." Gannon sat facing me, his right arm propped on the back of the couch, fingers lightly brushing over my shoulder.

"But?"

He chuckled.

"*But*," he started. "I ended up falling for this sexy little holiday helper." He held up a hand to stop my protest. "*And* fell for this town despite every effort not to. It will take a long time to work through the guilt and regret of not being here for my grandpa, I know that. And I'm completely at risk of becoming a holiday romance movie cliché."

I took his hand, my thumb brushing over his knuckles. "The part of the small-town transplant who blows into town determined not to care and ends up living happily ever after in love will now be played by Gannon Snow."

"I'm not sure I deserve a happily ever after—do those truly exist outside of romance novels and movies?—but I want to be a part of this place. Part of *you*, if you'll have me."

"Happily ever after *can* happen and we'll just live our own little romance novel. You deserve all the good, Gannon. Just let the magic do its work."

Gannon snorted. "Magic."

"Magic or eggnog," I taunted, waving my cup under his nose.

"Oh god, don't make me choose." Then he grimaced. "But I might take both of them over that damn train."

I cocked my head to hear the faint sound of the train whistle. "Think you can learn to live with it?"

"If it means having you by my side, I can learn to live with anything."

The day before Christmas, I convinced Gannon to take me into the city for a date so we could prove we had something outside of the holiday magic.

We definitely did.

But I was thrilled to get back home.

We spent Christmas Eve with my parents at The Heart hosting a party with goodies for the kids and last-minute shopping. Gannon was such a natural when it came to helping others—there was no doubt in my mind he'd inherited the skill from Joseph and I adored watching him in his element.

Christmas morning, we woke wrapped in each other's arms for what quickly became my very best Christmas to date.

"I'll give you one of your gifts tonight," I whispered suggestively. "But I got you something else. Open it before we head into town."

Gannon took the little box from me, but held it on his lap as he handed me a box. "I'm hoping we were going fairly small and nothing fancy this year," he said with a shy smile. "Open yours first in case mine is a lot less than what you got me."

Laughing, knowing there'd never be a gift as special as just having Gannon with me to celebrate Christmas, I tore into the package.

Simple navy-blue socks, bowtie, and suspenders lay on one side of the box. On the other were black socks with rabbits, wands, and top hats, and a matching bowtie and suspenders.

"I peeked through your collection and didn't see any like them. The navy is because it reminds me of your eyes. The magic ones are just because..." Gannon blushed as I cocked a brow, "...not saying I actually believe in the magic just yet, but finding you was definitely magical."

"Oh god, we have to leave, but if you keep talking like that, I'm going to jump you right here," I said, kissing him softly.

"No, no, I have to open a gift and we have to go in for the holiday thingy," Gannon said, opening his gift. He smiled as he swirled the snow in the snow globe. "It's Saint Nicholas Crossing," he said as he studied the custom-made globe with a train, trees, hill, old house, and town.

"Just no shaking it up unless you want to test the whole magic and snow globe weather theories."

Gannon's phone chimed and he picked it up. "Merry Christmas."

"Merry Christmas to you," a female voice said on the other end. "Since I haven't heard from you in a bit, I'm assuming it's safe to say you're staying?"

"Like you didn't do your best to orchestrate exactly that," Gannon said with a smirk.

"What? Me? Orchestrate? No," Ellen said and even I could hear the smile in her words.

"Mmhm," Gannon said. "Oh, how's the mold?"

Ellen full-on belly laughed. "Um, the mold turned out to be no big deal. Fake news."

"Exactly what I thought. You're sneaky and ruthless. You made me think I was homeless there for a minute."

"Nah," Ellen said. "I knew you just needed a push to figure out where your *real* home was."

"You already have my apartment sold?"

"No, but I did want to talk to you about that. Say the word and I'll have it done."

"We'll need a place for when we come visit," Gannon said, leaning over and pressing a kiss to my temple.

"No worries, I have plans for that as well."

"I trust you. Take care of it, please."

"I'll need an address for where I can ship your things," Ellen said.

Gannon glanced at me and I took his phone with glee. "Hi, Ellen. It's Hayden, nice to meet you." I rattled off my address and told her she was welcome to visit any time before handing the phone back to Gannon.

Later, at the town festival, as Gannon pulled me close to his side while we sipped hot chocolate and listened to the last songs of the carolers for the season, he took a deep breath.

"Everything good?" I asked. Perhaps I'd always worry he'd one day decide it wasn't enough, but talking about it wasn't ever going to be a bad thing.

"All good." Gannon kissed the top of my head. "Just thinking about how much Grandpa always talked about Christmas Day being so special here. I never really got to spend the holiday with him, but I know he loved it." He gestured at the light snow flurries. "I always swore I'd never come back and here I am enjoying carols and snow and hot chocolate."

I cuddled closer.

"I wasn't even *looking* for this, but here I am, more content and connected than ever. First Christmas of my adult life—hell, maybe of my entire life—I can remember being happy." Gannon tipped my chin. "And I owe it all to you."

"I think it's more than just me," I said against his cold lips. "This place, your grandpa, *the magic*. I was only a small part."

Gannon shook his head. "Without you, I likely never would have slowed down enough to even realize how different this place makes me. Being with you made me pause long enough to see where I belonged."

When the town festivities came to an end, we spent a couple hours with my parents before making our way back up to my little apartment. I wasn't sure how long Gannon would be content in the garage apartment, but it wasn't something we needed to discuss just yet.

Gannon showered while I prepared his Christmas gift.

Later, after I'd showered and prepped more of his Christmas gift, I walked out of the bathroom in a robe.

Gannon eyed me suspiciously, but only wrapped me in a hug under the mistletoe. "I didn't want to say it back the other day in the truck because it felt like I was just saying it because you did," he said. "I love you." He bent and kissed me. "I love you for how you take care of others. I love you for giving me a cute, sappy, sexy gay romance book to read and insisting we could get our very own happily ever after." Gannon pressed his forehead to mine. "I love how much you love this place and how you believe in the magic around you. I love your fashion accessories, your love for your students, all you do for the store, and how you knew I needed to make the decision to stay on my own without interference from you." He kissed me again. "I love you."

I cupped his cheeks in my hands. "I remember saying you were needed here for more than just the shop, the house, and finding closure with Joseph. I said maybe you were what would set a miracle into motion—you were here because the universe wanted it that way." Leaning in, I nuzzled my nose against his. "And I was right, but it was also because I needed you here. I needed you here to support my cheery giving and force me to take time for myself. I needed you to make me realize it was okay to want someone to love me. Could I have eventually done those things on my own? Yeah, but you made them all the better."

Gannon's hands ran up and down my back. "I needed you too. Needed this place. Both gave me a purpose—made me feel truly part of something. Wanted. Loved. My arrival here may have been what set the miracle into motion, but you— this thing between us—is the true miracle in our story."

We stood wrapped in each other's arms, savoring the moment.

"Do you want your Christmas present?" I asked, biting my lip nervously.

"Of course, especially if it involves you taking off that robe."

"Get naked and lie in the middle of the bed," I said.

Gannon stripped from his t-shirt and flannel pants, his long, thick cock already hard as he took his place on the mattress.

"Remember when you told me about your fantasy of me in just a jock with the bowtie and suspenders?" I asked.

"Holy fuck," Gannon growled. "Did you…"

Opening the neck of the robe to reveal a bowtie, I winked. Untying the sash as I walked toward the bed, I pulled the robe from my shoulders just enough to show the suspenders I wore.

Gannon reached for me and tried to pull me closer, but I smacked his hand away. "Hang on, greedy. You've got to see the whole outfit, be patient."

He laughed and gestured for me to continue as he stroked himself.

Dropping the robe, I stood completely on display for the man I loved.

I knew I looked the perfect mix of ridiculous and hot.

The black jock, black bowtie, and black suspenders, all made of faux leather—and likely something I'd never wear again unless Gannon wanted to play—fit me well and were a nice contrast to my pale skin.

I snapped the suspenders, pressing my lips together when the movement zinged through my nipples. Turning in a slow circle, knowing my ass looked damn good cupped in the jock straps, I finally made my way back around to face Gannon.

"What do you want?" I asked.

"Grab the lube, get your ass on my cock, and pull that pretty dick of yours out so you can come all over me," Gannon demanded.

Well then.

Wasting no time, thrilled Gannon had reacted just like I'd hoped, I grabbed the lube from the drawer and tossed it his way.

After climbing onto the bed, I gathered lube from Gannon's cock as he slicked himself and smeared it over my hole. Straddling his waist, I reached behind me to guide his swollen cockhead to my entrance.

Gannon cursed, gripping my thighs as he watched me above him, breathing out harshly with each inch of his cock I took into my tight heat. "So fucking hot," he gritted out. "Fucking sexy enough for a magazine, but all mine." He waited until I'd bottomed out and then trailed fingers up and down the suspenders. Snapping them against my bare chest, he grinned wickedly at my breathy gasp when the material made contact with my nipples. "Show me your cock and then hands on your head. Ride me so I can watch my boyfriend fuck his pretty little ass on my cock while he's all dressed up."

Pulling the front of the jock to the side, I fisted my cock, stroking slowly as I leaked onto Gannon's abdomen.

"Hands up and ride me," Gannon said.

With my hands clasped behind my head, the suspenders teasing over my nipples and sending shockwaves of pleasure through me, I rode Gannon in a slow, easy rhythm. Each grind and roll of my hips had his cock brushing over my prostate, my dick throbbing as pre-cum dripped from the head, and my ass clenching in anticipation of my orgasm.

"Fuck, Hayden. So damn hot and tight. Look at you, baby," Gannon murmured as he reached for my hips and held me tight to him as he thrust up into me hard and fast. "Gonna come, fuck, gonna come."

Gannon cried out as he shot his load deep in my ass just as I brought my hands down to dig into his chest and ride out my release, the tight muscle of my ass gripping his pulsing cock.

Just when I thought he'd pull out of me, Gannon rolled us so I was on my back and thrust into me over and over, pushing his cum deeper with each press of his hips.

"I love you so damn much," he muttered against my lips. "And no one else sees this outfit but me. I don't care when else you put it on, but I want this as my Christmas present every fucking year."

I laughed. "Easiest Christmas gift ever."

"*Best* Christmas gift ever," Gannon said at my ear.

And I knew he wasn't just talking about the bowtie and suspenders.

Epilogue

GANNON

Two Years Later

"Look at my guy," Hayden murmured in my ear as we helped a family shop for Christmas. "Mr. Christmas Town himself."

I chuckled and hefted the toddler on my hip a bit higher so she could look at the dolls one shelf too high for her. "That's me. Maybe we should think about a calendar."

Hayden giggled, but the waggle of his brow told me he wasn't completely against the idea. Ever since I'd decided to stay in St. Nicholas Crossing, Hayden and I had been a top-notch team when it came to dreaming big and putting plans in place to make our town—and The Heart—bigger and better for our citizens.

We had about fifteen minutes before the holiday party at the store was scheduled to start and I was about to sweat through my dress shirt and festive sweater.

Yeah, Hayden had me going all-in when it came to holiday cheer these days.

I helped with the Christmas pageant, the shop, decorations. You name it, I probably had a hand in it. My business was thriving—both the LA location and the new Midwest location. And while we'd enjoyed a couple trips to LA over the last two years, I'd quickly realized I'd never be bored in St. Nicholas Crossing.

As for LA, it was no longer home.

Hayden had enjoyed the warmth, but the sun was not friendly to his skin even after layers of sunscreen.

And I found myself annoyed with the city overall. Crowded, smoggy, and just wastefully materialistic when compared to St. Nicholas Crossing.

Our next trip to the west coast would likely take us sightseeing outside of LA, there was so much beauty to explore and I wanted to be by Hayden's side as he experienced it.

As the last family left the shopping area, I cleared my throat to gather folks near the register. Hayden had no idea what was about to happen and I congratulated myself on keeping everything under wraps when my boyfriend was the nosiest little snoop in town.

After waiting for the buzz of conversation to die down, I gave everyone a smile. "Thanks for being here. I know the pageant starts soon and I won't keep you long." I shook a few hands of people I'd come to consider friends and took a deep breath before turning to Hayden.

"Two years ago, I learned that Joseph Snow had promised this place to the town for a period of two Christmases. If it made a profit both years, the town could keep The Heart. If not, it would be mine to do with as I wished."

Hayden tensed beside me. He saw the books daily and I knew he was aware the past year hadn't been where we'd hoped as far as profitability.

"Two years ago, I said I'd make a business decision based on facts and numbers, not on feelings—we're a business, not just a charity. If this place wasn't bringing in money, we'd sell because, like it or not, a business that doesn't make money isn't helping anyone." I pulled a piece of paper from my pocket. "I've run the numbers and unfortunately, we're going to be short."

Hayden's face fell.

"I don't care about being short by," I paused and looked at the paper, "just ten dollars because I know the good The Heart does for people. But I'm a business man at heart and keeping a place based on feelings just isn't a smart move. So, we're going to have to sell."

Shock, hurt, and anger filled Hayden's face, but I pushed on quickly.

Taking his hand, I said, "Hayden, I wanted to give you the first chance to buy because I know how much The Heart means to you."

Hayden glanced around nervously. "Babe," he muttered. "You know I don't have that type of money. Maybe we should talk—"

"Asking price is a dollar," I said with a smile. "Would you like to buy?"

Hayden looked confused for a moment before his face brightened. "For real? You're selling me this place for one dollar?"

I nodded.

Hayden dug a dollar from his pocket and handed it to me.

As I stuffed the bill in my own pocket, I pulled out a velvet box and dropped to one knee.

Hayden's eyes went wide and he put a hand to his mouth.

"Two years ago, I fell for a sexy, cheery little holiday helper with the cutest bowtie and suspender collection, the most adorable windblown hair, freckles, and kissable mouth."

Pretty sure both our cheeks turned pink at the mention of suspenders, bowties, and kissable mouths.

"But I fell for real when I realized what a generous,

caring, happy spirit you were." I reached for his hand. "Hayden, if you'll have me, I want to spend the rest of my life supporting you, helping you help others, and making sure you take time for yourself as well." I looked up at him, my heart in my throat. "Will you marry me?"

Hayden nodded, tears shining in his eyes as he yanked me up to stand with him and let me slip the ring on his finger. "Yes," he mumbled against my mouth, our lips a mixture of smiles, laughter, and kisses. "The cold? The snow? The train? You're sure?"

"I'd marry you a thousand times despite that damn train," I said with a sheepish shrug. "I barely notice it at all anymore."

"And the magic?" Hayden teased.

"Nope, not going to get me on that one."

"We'll work on it," he said with a wink.

Two More Years Later

The weather for our winter wedding couldn't have been more perfect.

Hayden had offered spring, summer, or fall for our special day, but I knew he wanted a holiday wedding.

So, we set plans into motion and here we were on the Wednesday after Christmas—what? As a store owner and teacher, Hayden's schedule was pretty booked. There was nothing wrong with a Wednesday wedding, especially in a beautiful little small town with the sun shining brightly on a sparkling white layer of freshly fallen snow.

Did a tiny part of me want to believe, maybe just for a second, that the gentle shake I'd given my St. Nicholas Crossing snow globe along with muttered words indicating we'd really appreciate a bit of snow and beautiful winter weather had something to do with the gorgeous picture before me?

Maybe.

But don't tell my husband to be.

Speaking of Hayden, my breath caught in my throat as we each rounded a corner of Joseph's big wrap-around porch and our eyes met.

My man was so damn gorgeous.

Dark gray suit with navy accents. He wore the bowtie, suspenders, and socks I'd gotten him all those years ago.

The *other* bowtie and suspenders—certain black leather ones—had once again been put to fabulous use on Christmas Day before being tucked away for the next time we wanted to play. No jock and accessories had ever been so appreciated.

Hayden's hair, which I'd finally decided simply had a mind of its own, fluttered in the light winter wind.

More than looking amazing, this man was beautiful on the inside too.

He'd taken his role as store owner very seriously once all the paperwork had been sorted, and The Heart had increased profits over the past two years.

Hayden still taught only part-time, insisting he wanted to be available for the shop as well.

Most of my time was spent in meetings with Ellen and our team—I pretty much just sat back and watched my businesses grow with great people working for me—and doing whatever needed to be done at The Heart.

Restoring bits and pieces of Joseph's old house also kept me busy and I found myself chatting with him—or the urn of his ashes—throughout each little project I took on around the old place.

We'd moved up to the hill house around the same time we got engaged. Hayden's parents had kept the garage apartment empty for us "just in case" for a while, but they were now offering it as temporary housing for those in need.

Hayden smiled at me as he took my hands in his. "Did you wish for this weather with your snow globe?" he teased.

"I'll never tell," I answered with a smile and a wink.

"Gentlemen, are we ready?" the officiant asked. "I believe you both wrote something?"

I cleared my throat. "I'll start because I don't want to have to follow whatever this one has to say."

The small group of guests chuckled.

Hoping I wouldn't forget what I wanted to say, I gripped Hayden's hands and started. "We fell hard and quick and it maybe shouldn't have worked out, but the universe had other ideas. This place is my home—always has been, despite me fighting against it—but without you, it would just be a place. *You* are my heart, my home, my happily ever after and I vow to spend the rest of my life making sure you know you're loved and taken care of just as much as you love and take care of others."

Hayden dashed away a tear. "Well, now I guess *I* get to follow that." He sniffled and took a deep breath. "The first time I saw you, I was a kid infatuated with the gorgeous, mysterious, older guy. The second time I saw you, I said a quick thank you to the universe, the magic, fate, whoever was listening. I knew immediately I wanted to know you more." He gave my hands a squeeze. "I learned quickly that you used money and success to close off and protect your heart, you put up walls to distance yourself from emotions. But the more I watched you sink into the welcoming arms of this place, the more you learned the warmth of giving and how good it feels to be needed, wanted, and loved, I knew the magic was at work."

I cleared my throat. "I prefer to believe that was *you* and what we found together, not the magic."

Hayden smirked. "The part of my skeptical *husband* will now be played by Gannon Snow. And we'll keep working on the magic. One of these days, you'll believe."

As the train whistle sounded in the distance, I married the love of my life. Did the universe have a hand in our happily ever after? Fate? Magic?

We may never know.

But with Hayden by my side and love in my heart, one thing's for certain...

I *believe*.

Want to read *Holly Hills Christmas* and enjoy the story of Kota and Vince? Click HERE. Or check out *Listen to Your Heart*, another Christmas romance by A.D. Ellis, HERE.

Not in the mood for holiday romance? Find all of A.D. Ellis's other M/M romances HERE.

Also by A.D. Ellis

Holly Hills Christmas- Holly Hills Christmas is a steamy, feel-good, M/M age-gap holiday romance.

Listen to Your Heart- a steamy, second chance, M/M romance with just enough holiday magic to make you believe. It shares the same world with Follow Your Heart by Declan Rhodes.

Jett & Leighton: On Cravenwood Block- a steamy, opposites-attract, bisexual-awakening, roommates-to-lovers M/M romance featuring a sexy-as-sin tattoo artist and a fresh, flashy barista with a smile that lights up the room.

Ollie & Bash: On Cravenwood Block- a steamy, opposites-attract, roommates-to-lovers, boss/employee, age-gap M/M romance featuring a man not looking for love and a younger music director with no filter.

Julian & Shaw: On Cravenwood Block- a steamy, hurt/comfort, roommates-to-lovers, age-gap M/M romance featuring an apartment manager with a heart of gold and a younger man doing his best to heal from a traumatic past.

Lucas & Dean: On Cravenwood Block- a steamy, friends-to-lovers, bisexual awakening M/M romance featuring lifelong best friends.

The Perfect Blend- A steamy, M/M age-gap, marriage of convenience, coffee shop romance

Perfect Timing is a steamy, M/M romance with an introverted, demisexual writer and a big, soft teddy bear of a nurse trying to navigate a love they've always dreamed of but most definitely weren't expecting.

Adore (Remington Place 1) is a steamy, age-gap, bi-awakening, dad's best friend M/M romance with a sassy smartass and a sexy silver fox. It's the first book in the Remington Place series and can be read as a stand-alone.

Crave (Remington Place 2) is a steamy, friends-to-lovers, fake relationship M/M romance with a virgin nursing student and a gruff, grumbly construction worker.

Desire (Remington Place 3) is a steamy, age-gap, hurt/comfort M/M romance featuring a heart-of-gold mechanic and a twink who's a lot stronger than he realizes. *Please note: This story has mention of sex trafficking and sexual abuse.*

Yearn (Remington Place 4)- a steamy, enemies-to-lovers, forced proximity M/M romance between two EMS workers who have hated each other for a decade.

Power Struggle is a steamy M/M, age-gap, forced proximity romance set in a small town. A twenty-year history, rival schools and jobs, and a hotel with only one bed make for a hot and heavy, sweet and sexy, HEA-guaranteed love story.

Take Me Home M/M age-gap, opposites-attract romance with plenty of steam and a scene that will make you appreciate camouflage and work boots

Let Love In M/M age-gap, forced proximity, dad's best friend, bisexual-awakening romance. Available on AUDIO!

Let Love Win M/M brother's best friend romance. Available on AUDIO!

Buried Secrets Romantic suspense stand-alone title. Available on AUDIO!

Silver in the City (3 books- meet the Silver crew you read about in Forged in the City) Available on AUDIO!

Forged in the City (3 books- a spin-off series from Silver in the City) Available on AUDIO

The BJ Boys Series (3 books, small town, big love) Available on AUDIO

Forever Better Together (friends to lovers) Available on AUDIO!

His Reluctant Cowboy (age gap, opposites attract, cowboy romance) Available on AUDIO!

What Blooms Beneath (LGBT Fantasy romance) Available on AUDIO!

Sawyer

(this was the first M/M I wrote and you may remember Sawyer and Luke being mentioned in Barrett & Ivan as well as in Ryker & Gavin)

The Something About Him series has been revamped with revised stories, updated blurbs, and spiffy new covers.

The series is available on ALL of your favorite book platforms!

Bryan & Jase

Brody & Nick

Barrett & Ivan

Braeton & Drew

Ryker & Gavin

Kade & Cameron

Acknowledgments

It's always so hard to write this part because I'm worried I'll forget someone without meaning to.

Readers- you are the reason I write. As long as you continue reading my stories, I'll continue writing them. Thank you for your support.

Bloggers- your support, reviews, and promotion are very much appreciated. Thank you!

My author buddies- I don't know that I could keep doing this without our brainstorm sessions, laughter, road trips, meals, wine, and friendship as my support.

Thank you to my alpha readers, betas, editors, proofreaders, and ARC readers! Your eyes and input are beyond important to me.

Brett and Gage- as usual, I doubt you even grasp how much your support, input, and friendship mean to me. This author journey has brought many wonderful things into my life, and you both are two of the BEST! I'm blessed to call you friends.

My family and friends- thank you for your love and support, always.

About the Author

A.D. Ellis is an Indiana girl, born and raised. She spends much of her time in central Indiana as an instructional coach/teacher in the inner city of Indianapolis, being a mom to two amazing teenagers, and wondering how she and her husband of over two decades haven't driven each other insane yet. A lot of her time is also devoted to phone call avoidance and her hatred of cooking.

She loves chocolate, wine, pizza, and naps along with reading and writing romance. These loves don't leave much time for housework, much to the chagrin of her husband. Who would pick cleaning the house over a nap or a good book? She uses any extra time to increase her fluency in sarcasm.

A.D. uses she/they pronouns.

Sign up at http://www.subscribepage.com/ADEllisNewsMMRomance for a FREE books!

Website http://adellisauthor.com/

Find me EVERYWHERE at https://www.adellisauthor.com/mylinks/

Copyright © 2022 by A.D. Ellis

All rights reserved.

No part of this book may be reproduced in any form or by any electronic or
mechanical means, including information storage and retrieval systems,
without written permission from the author, except for the use of brief
quotations in a book review.

www.ingramcontent.com/pod-product-compliance
Lightning Source LLC
Chambersburg PA
CBHW020812060726
47498CB00017B/2768